The Merchant of Venice

威尼斯商人

Original Author	William Shakespeare
Adaptor	David Desmond O'Flaherty
Illustrator	Gutdva lrina Mixailovna

WORDS
600

MP3

Let's Enjoy Masterpieces!

All the beautiful fairy tales and masterpieces that you have encountered during your childhood remain as warm memories in your adulthood. This time, let's indulge in the world of masterpieces through English. You can enjoy the depth and beauty of original works, which you can't enjoy through Chinese translations.

The stories are easy for you to understand because of your familiarity with them. When you enjoy reading, your ability to understand English will also rapidly improve.

This series of *Let's Enjoy Masterpieces* is a special reading comprehension booster program, devised to improve reading comprehension for beginners whose command of English is not satisfactory, or who are elementary, middle, and high school students. With this program, you can enjoy reading masterpieces in English with fun and efficiency.

This carefully planned program is composed of 5 levels, from the beginner level of 350 words to the intermediate and advanced levels of 1,000 words. With this program's level-by-level system, you are able to read famous texts in English and to savor the true pleasure of the world's language.

The program is well conceived, composed of reader-friendly explanations of English expressions and grammar, quizzes to help the student learn vocabulary and understand the meaning of the texts, and fabulous illustrations that adorn every page. In addition, with our "Guide to Listening," not only is reading comprehension enhanced but also listening comprehension skills are highlighted.

In the audio recording of the book, texts are vividly read by professional American actors. The texts are rewritten, according to the levels of the readers by an expert editorial staff of native speakers, on the basis of standard American English with the ministry of education recommended vocabulary. Therefore, it will be of great help even for all the students that want to learn English.

Please indulge yourself in the fun of reading and listening to English through *Let's Enjoy Masterpieces*.

莎士比亞 William Shakespeare (1564–1616)

The world's greatest playwright, William Shakespeare, was born of a middle class family in England. Since his family had money, his childhood was very comfortable. However, William could not attend a university, because his family lost their wealth when he was thirteen years old.

At the age of eighteen he married Anne Hathaway, who was eight years older than him. He had three children with her.

It is believed that Shakespeare began to write as a playwright around 1590. In the beginning, he was just copying the stories of other authors and sharpening his writing skills. But he kept getting more and more popular. Finally, he achieved some success as an actor and a playwright and in 1594 became a leading member of the King's official playwright company, where he continued to write until his death.

He wrote thirty-seven plays, and his work is generally divided up into four periods: historic plays, "joyous" comedies, tragedies, and tragic romantic comedies. His four well-known great tragedies include *Hamlet*, *Othello*, *King Lear*, and *Macbeth*. They were written during the tragedies period. The sonnets in Shakespeare's plays clearly support his reputation as the best poet and greatest dramatist that has ever lived.

Shakespeare died on his fifty-second birthday on April 23, 1616 in his birthplace, Stratford-Upon-Avon. The people there still annually celebrate his death.

The Merchant of Venice is a comedy divided up into five acts and was published in 1597. Antonio, a Venetian merchant, has a close friend, Bassanio. One day, Bassanio asks Antonio for a loan because he desperately needs money to court Portia, who lives in Belmont.

Antonio agrees, but he is unable to make the loan himself, so he borrows some money at an exorbitant interest rate from the moneylender Shylock. The moneylender will also be entitled to a pound of Antonio's own flesh if he can't pay back the loan.

In order to marry Portia, Bassanio must first choose the case that contains her portrait from among the three different cases made of gold, silver, and lead. He passes the test and gets a chance to marry her.

In the meantime, Antonio has lost all of his ships and can no longer pay back the loan from Shylock. Wise Portia hears of this and disguises herself as a man and becomes Antonio's lawyer. Finally, she saves him with her wisdom.

She reminds Shylock that he can take a pound of Antonio's flesh only if he can do it without causing any bleeding because the contract does not entitle him to spill any blood.

The Merchant of Venice is one of Shakespeare's romantic comedies and is the most popular and successful work among his comic plays.

HOW TO USE THIS BOOK
本書使用說明

1 *Original English texts*

It is easy to understand the meaning of the text, because the text is divided phrase by phrase and sentence by sentence.

2 *Explanation of the vocabulary*

The words and expressions that include vocabulary above the elementary level are clearly defined.

3 *Response notes*

Spaces are included in the book so you can take notes about what you don't understand or what you want to remember.

4 *One point lesson*

In-depth analyses of major grammar points and expressions help you to understand sentences with difficult grammar.

🎧 Audio Recording

In the audio recording, native speakers narrate the texts in standard American English. By combining the written words and the audio recording, you can listen to English with great ease.

Audio books have been popular in Britain and America for many decades. They allow the listener to experience the proper word pronunciation and sentence intonation that add important meaning and drama to spoken English. Students will benefit from listening to the recording twenty or more times.

After you are familiar with the text and recording, listen once more with your eyes closed to check your listening comprehension. Finally, after you can listen with your eyes closed and understand every word and every sentence, you are then ready to mimic the native speaker.

Then you should make a recording by reading the text yourself. Then play both recordings to compare your oral skills with those of a native speaker.

HOW TO IMPROVE
READING ABILITY
如何增進英文閱讀能力

① *Catch key words*

Read the key words in the sentences and practice catching the gist of the meaning of the sentence. You might question how working with a few important words could enhance your reading ability. However, it's quite effective. If you continue to use this method, you will find out that the key words and your knowledge of people and situations enables you to understand the sentence.

② *Divide long sentences*

Read in chunks of meaning, dividing sentences into meaningful chunks of information. In the book, chunks are arranged in sentences according to meaning. If you consider the sentences backwards or grammatically, your reading speed will be slow and you will find it difficult to listen to English.

You are ready to move to a more sophisticated level of comprehension when you find that narrowly focusing on chunks is irritating. Instead of considering the chunks, you will make it a habit to read the sentence from the beginning to the end to figure out the meaning of the whole.

❸ Make inferences and assumptions

Making inferences and assumptions is part of your ability. If you don't know, try to guess the meaning of the words. Although you don't know all the words in context, don't go straight to the dictionary. Developing an ability to make inferences in the context is important.

The first way to figure out the meaning of a word is from its context. If you cannot make head or tail out of the meaning of a word, look at what comes before or after it. Ask yourself what can happen in such a situation. Make your best guess as to the word's meaning. Then check the explanations of the word in the book or look up the word in a dictionary.

❹ Read a lot and reread the same book many times

There is no shortcut to mastering English. Only if you do a lot of reading will you make your way to the summit. Read fun and easy books with an average of less than one new word per page. Try to immerse yourself in English as often as you can.

Spend time "swimming" in English. Language learning research has shown that immersing yourself in English will help you improve your English, even though you may not be aware of what you're learning.

CONTENTS

Before You Read

Shylock

I am a moneylender[1] living in Venice, Italy. I make[2] a lot of money by lending money to others and charging[3] them high interest[4]. People in Venice hate me because I am Jewish[5] and greedy[6]. But I don't care. I hate them, too, particularly[7], Antonio.

1. **moneylender** [`mʌniˌlendər] (n.) 放貸的人
2. **make money** 賺錢
3. **charge** [tʃɑːrdʒ] (v.) 索價；索費
4. **interest** [`ɪntərest] (n.) 利息
5. **Jewish** [`dʒuːɪʃ] (a.) 猶太人的
6. **greedy** [`gridi] (a.) 貪婪的
7. **particularly** [pərˈtikjələrli] (adv.) 特別地

Antonio

Like Shylock, I am a moneylender. I am, however, quite different from[1] him. I like helping people when they are in trouble[2]. I often lend money to others and don't charge any interest. Shylock hates me for doing this. I hate him, too, because he is heartless[3] and greedy.

1. **be different from** 與……不相同
2. **be in trouble** 在困難中；有難
3. **heartless** [`hɑːrtləs] (a.) 無情的；冷酷的

12

Bassanio

I am Antonio's best friend. Whenever I need money, Antonio helps me. Recently, I fell in love with[1] a wonderful woman named Portia. I need some money to buy Portia some gifts before I propose to[2] her. As always, I will ask Antonio to help me.

1. **to fall in love with sb** 愛上某人   2. **to propose to sb** 向某人求婚

Portia

My father recently passed away[1], and I inherited[2] a lot of money. Before he died, he set up[3] some conditions[4] for suitors[5] who want to marry me. They must go through[6] a test.

1. **to pass away** 過世
2. **inherit** [in`herɪt] (v.) 繼承
3. **to set up** 設立
4. **condition** [kən`dɪʃən] (n.) 條件
5. **suitor** [`sutər] (n.) 求婚者
6. **to go through** 通過

Gratiano and Nerissa

We are Bassanio and Portia's servants[1]. Even though[2] we are inferior to[3] them, they treat us like[4] their own family. We will always be loyal to[5] them.

1. **servant** [`sɜ:rvənt] (n.) 僕役
2. **even though** 即使
3. **be inferior to sb** 地位較低的
4. **to treat sb like** 待某人如……
5. **be loyal to sb** 對某人忠誠

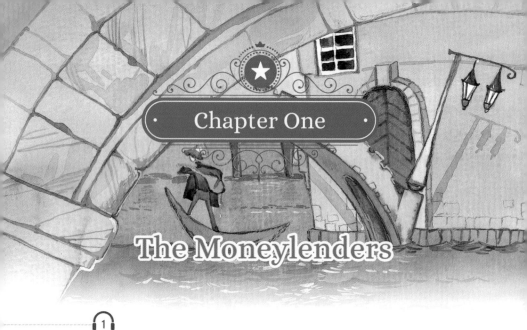

Chapter One

The Moneylenders

I have a story to tell. It is a story of love and hatred. A story of giving and taking. A story of laughter and tears. This story was told a long time ago. But it still has as much meaning today as it did then.

It happened in a city called Venice[1] in Italy. This beautiful city rests[2] like a crown[3] jewel[4] on the Adriatic Sea[5].

1. **Venice** [`vɛnɪs] (n.)
   義大利城市威尼斯
2. **rest** [rɛst] (v.)
   擺放;放置在……上
3. **crown** [kraʊn] (n.) 皇冠
4. **jewel** [`dʒuːəl] (n.)
   寶石;珠寶
5. **Adriatic Sea** 亞得里亞海
   (義大利和巴爾幹半島間的內海)
6. **merchant** [`mɜːrtʃənt] (n.)
   商人
7. **repay** [rɪ`peɪ] (v.) 償還;回報
   (repay-repaid-repaid)
8. **in terrible ways** 以悽慘的方式
9. **simply** [`sɪmpli] (adv.)
   單純地;只是

There lived a moneylender named Shylock in Venice. He earned a lot by lending money to merchants[6].

Many people hated Shylock. Some people hated him because he forced merchants to repay[7] him in terrible ways[8]. Others hated him simply[9] because he was Jewish.

Of all the merchants who lived in Venice, one hated Shylock more than the others. His name was Antonio.

Shylock hated Antonio as well[1]. This was because Antonio was a very generous moneylender. He lent money to people in trouble and often didn't charge them interest. Shylock lost a lot of business because of Antonio's generosity[2].

1. **as well** 也
2. **generosity** [ˌdʒenəˈrɑːsəti] (n.) 慷慨；寬宏大量
3. **Christian** [ˈkrɪstʃən] (n.) 基督徒
4. **Jew** [dʒuː] (n.) 猶太人
5. **in those days** 在以前
6. **agree about sth** 同意某事
7. **religion** [rɪˈlɪdʒən] (n.) 宗教
8. **culture** [ˈkʌltʃər] (n.) 文化
9. **run into sb** 巧遇某人

More importantly, Shylock hated Antonio because he was a Christian[3]. And Antonio hated Shylock because he was a Jew[4]. In those days[5], Jews and Christians didn't like each other. They couldn't agree about[6] anything. They couldn't understand each other's religion[7] or culture[8].

Antonio and Shylock often ran into[9] each other at the Rialto[10]. The Rialto was the business center[11] of Venice. When the two met, they would have arguments[12]. Antonio would often yell at[13] Shylock for the heartless way of doing business[14]. Shylock often thought about[15] ways to get even with[16] Antonio.

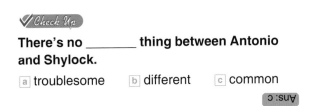

✔ Check Up

There's no _____ thing between Antonio and Shylock.

a troublesome   b different   c common

Ans: c

10. **rialto** [rɪˋæltou] (n.) 威尼斯市中心、財政金融中心
11. **business center** 商業中心
12. **argument** [ˋɑːrgument] (n.) 爭論；爭吵（動詞 argue）
13. **yell at sb** 對某人吼叫；叫罵
14. **do business** 做事業
15. **think about sth** 思考某事
16. **get even with sb** 對某人施以報復

Almost everyone in Venice really liked Antonio. They felt that he was kind and honest. The merchants especially admired[1] him. They knew that he would help them when they were in hard times[2].

Antonio's best friend was a young man named Bassanio. Bassanio's family was very rich. His parents had given him money, but Bassanio had spent it all. He had wasted his money on[3] wine and good food. He had traveled and he had had fun[4]. And, of course, he ended up[5] without any money. This was very common[6] for young men during that time[7].

In the past[8], Antonio had helped him in many ways. In fact, he already owed[9] Antonio lots of money.

1. **admire** [əd`maɪr] (v.)
   讚賞;佩服;欽佩
2. **in hard times** 艱困期
3. **waste money on. . .**
   把錢揮霍在……
4. **have fun** 玩得快樂
5. **end up** 到頭來;結果
6. **common** [`kɑ:mən] (a.)
   普遍的;常見的
7. **during that time**
   在那個時候
8. **in the past** 過去;以往
9. **owe sb sth** 欠某人某事
10. **share sth with sb**
    與某人分享某事某物

Antonio never said "no" to Bassanio.
It seemed Antonio was happy to share[10] his
money with his friends.

One day, Bassanio came to Antonio for[1] another loan[2].

"Antonio! I have great news! I've fallen in love with someone! Her name is Portia. She's the most beautiful woman in the world! And not only that[3], she's rich, too. Her father passed away recently, and she's going to inherit lots of money!"

"That's wonderful news, Bassanio," said Antonio. "It sounds like she is a wonderful woman, but does she love you as much as you love her?"

"Of course, she does. When she looks at me, her eyes are full of[4] love and respect. Listen. I want to buy some gifts for her. The only problem is that[5] I don't have any money right now. I know I owe you a lot of money, but can I borrow a little more? I promise I'll pay you back[6]."

1. **come to sb for sth** 為某事前來找某人
2. **loan** [loun] (n.) 借錢；貸款（可是借款或放款）
3. **and not only that** 而且不止如此
4. **be full of** 充滿
5. **the only problem is that** 唯一的問題是……
6. **pay back** 償還

🎧 5

　　"Bassanio! You know that my money is your money. I'd gladly[1] lend it to you anytime. The only problem is that I don't have any money right now. I've spent all of my money on merchandise[2]. I can't help you. I'm sorry."

　　"What should I do?" asked Bassanio. "She'll never marry me unless I give her some gifts."

1. **gladly** [`glædli] (adv.)
　　高興地；欣然地
2. **merchandise**
　　[`mɜːrtʃənˌdaɪz] (n.)
　　商品；貨品
3. **on hand** 手頭上

4. **sign** [saɪn] (v.) 簽名；簽字
　　（名詞 signature）
5. **loan agreement** 借據
　　agreement 同意書；合約
6. **any day** 隨時；就快要

The Merchant of Venice

"Don't worry," said Antonio. "I know what you can do. You can borrow money from a moneylender named Shylock. He always has money on hand[3]. He'll certainly lend you money if I sign[4] a loan agreement[5]. And the ships will come in any day[6] now. I'll make lots of money when my merchandise arrives. I'll pay him back then."

"Thanks, Antonio. You really are a great friend!"

One Point Lesson

He'll certainly lend you money if I sign a loan agreement.
如果我簽下一紙借據的話，他一定會借錢給你。

假設句的標準句型：If + 主詞 + 動詞現在式，主詞 + will (can, may) + 動詞現在式

e.g. If I need money, I'll borrow some from Ken.
如果我缺錢，我會向肯借一點。

While Bassanio and Antonio were out to find Shylock, Portia was facing her own problems. Portia's father had arranged[1] conditions of her marriage before he died.

He didn't trust Portia's judgment[2]. He felt that she would choose an unsuitable[3] person to marry. So, before he died, he had put three chests[4] in a room. One chest was made of[5] gold, one of silver and one of lead[6]. In one of these chests was a small picture of Portia.

If a suitor chose the right box, he would find the picture. That meant that he could propose[7] to Portia. Portia's father believed that the best husband would know which box to choose.

If he found the wrong box, he would have to leave the house right away. He wouldn't be allowed[8] to marry Portia.

In addition[9], he wouldn't be able to[10] marry anyone or have a girlfriend for the rest of his life[11]. Every suitor had to sign a contract[12] agreeing to these conditions. It was a big risk[13] for them. But Portia's father felt that his daughter was worth[14] the risk.

1. **arrange** [əˋreɪndʒ] (v.) 安排
2. **judgment** [ˋdʒʌdʒmənt] (n.)
   判斷；判斷力
3. **unsuitable** [ʌnˋsuːtəbl̩] (a.)
   不適合的；不宜的
4. **chest** [tʃest] (n.)
   有蓋的大型箱子
5. **be made of** 用……做的
6. **lead** [led] (n.) 鉛
7. **propose** [prəˋpouz] (v.) 求婚

8. **be allowed to** 被允許；獲准
9. **in addition** 此外；還有
10. **be able to** 得以；能夠
11. **for the rest of one's life**
    終其一生
12. **contract** [ˋkɑːtræt] (n.) 契約
13. **risk** [rɪsk] (n.) 風險
14. **worth + n./Ving**
    值得……或值得做……

Portia lived in a small town called "Belmont." She had many men visit her house. They all wanted to marry her because she was rich and beautiful.

She was tired of[1] having these strange men come to her house. She was also unhappy that her father didn't trust her judgment. Portia often talked to her servant, Nerissa, about her problems. Nerissa was more of a friend than a servant.

"Why couldn't my father just trust[2] me?" she asked Nerissa one day.

"Your father was right," said Nerissa. "There are so many bad men out there. They just want to marry you for your money."

"But the men who come here are so boring[3]. They have bad manners[4], and they are vain[5]. Some of them drink too much wine. Some of them even smoke! Ah! I'm so sick of[6] these guys[7]!"

1. **be tired of** 厭煩
2. **trust** [trʌst] (v.) 信任
3. **boring** [`bɔːrɪŋ] (a.)
   乏味的；枯燥的
4. **manners** [`mænərz] (n.)
   禮貌；禮節
5. **vain** [veɪn] (a.)
   自負的；虛榮的
6. **be sick of** 厭倦
7. **guy** [gaɪ] (n.) 傢伙

One Point Lesson

She was also **unhappy** that her father didn't trust her judgment. 她也很難過，因為她的父親不信任她的判斷力。

unhappy : happy 的反義詞。英文中字首加上 un 即表示反義。im-、in-、dis- 等，也都表示為原字的反義詞。

e.g. It was **impossible** for him to help you at that moment. 那時要他去幫助你是不可能的（辦不到的）。

Portia was a very independent[1] person. She was capable of[2] making decisions[3] for herself. She also believed that she was smarter[4] than most men. Portia was sad. She thought that she would have to marry a boring, stupid man with bad habits[5].

"Not one of these guys is decent[6]. What should I do?"

"Do you remember the man from Venice?" asked Nerissa.

1. **independent** [ˌɪndɪˈpɛndənt] (a.) 獨立自主的
   反義詞：dependent 依賴的
2. **be capable of Ving** 有能力做
3. **make a decision** 做決定
4. **smart** [smɑːrt] (a.) 聰明機伶的
5. **bad habits** 壞習慣
6. **decent** [ˈdisənt] (a.) 正派的
7. **sparkle** [ˈspɑːrkl] (v.) 閃動光芒

Portia's eyes sparkled[7]. "Yes. I remember him. Bassanio. How could I forget? He was so much better than all of the other men who came here. He was handsome and gentle[8]. He was charming, kind, and intelligent[9]. But it's hopeless! He'll never sign my father's contract. I'm a woman who can't even choose her own husband. I'm so unlucky!"

Another servant then entered[10] the room. "Madam[11], a message[12] has arrived from the Prince of Morocco[13]. He will be arriving tomorrow."

"Great! Another unsuitable suitor! I wonder[14] what problems this one will have."

8. **gentle** [ˋdʒɛntl] (a.) 溫文的
9. **intelligent** [ɪnˋtɛlɪdʒənt] (a.) 聰明的
10. **enter** [ˋɛntər] (v.) 進入
11. **madam** [ˋmædəm] (n.) 女士；小姐；夫人
12. **message** [ˋmɛsɪdʒ] (n.) 口信；消息
13. **Morocco** [məˋrɑːkou] (n.) 摩洛哥
14. **wonder** [ˋwʌndər] (v.) 納悶；想知道

29

A Fill in the blanks with the given words.

religion merchandise decisions arguments loan

1 When Shylock and Antonio met, they would have

_____.

2 Jews and Christians couldn't understand each other's

_____.

3 Bassanio came to Antonio for another _____.

4 Antonio spent all of his money on _____.

5 Portia can make _____ for herself.

B Write down the persons who said the following words.

1 You know that my money is your money.

_____

2 I'm a woman who can't even choose her own husband.

_____

3 There are so many bad men out there.

_____

4 She'll never marry me unless I give her some gifts.

_____

C Choose the best answer to each question.

1 Why did merchants especially like Antonio?

(a) Because he was a Christian.

(b) Because he was rich and good-looking.

(c) Because he helped them when they were in trouble.

2 Why did Portia's father arrange the conditions of her marriage?

(a) Because he didn't want to give her his money.

(b) Because he didn't trust Portia's judgment.

(c) Because he was a very greedy man.

D Match the characters with the descriptions.

1 Shylock   **2** Portia   **3** Antonia

• • •

• • •

a independent   **b** heartless   **c** generous

Venice

Venice was founded[1] in 452 AD, when barbarians[2] invaded[3] Northern Italy. The Romans who lived in the cities of this area retreated[4] onto hundreds of small islands that lay just off the coast of the Adriatic Sea.

They built their houses and other buildings on wooden beams[5] called "pilings[6]." To connect the islands, they built hundreds of bridges. Most of these bridges are arched[7] so that boats can pass under them.

---

1. **found** [faʊnd] (v.) 建立；奠基
2. **barbarian** [bɑːrˋberiən] (n.)
   野蠻人；異族
3. **invade** [ɪnˋved] (v.) 侵略；入侵
4. **retreat** [rɪˋtrit] (v.) 撤退；退隱

5. **beam** [biːm] (v.) 樑
6. **piling** [ˋpaɪlɪŋ] (n.) 樁
7. **arch** [ɑːrtʃ] (v.) 使成拱形
8. **as a result** 結果
9. **waterway** [ˋwɔːtərwe] (n.) 水道；運河

As a result[8], many of the "streets" of Venice are actually waterways[9].

In 697 AD, these surviving[10] Romans formed[11] a republic[12]. The government encouraged commerce[13], and Venice soon developed[14] into an important commercial[15] hub[16].

Today, Venice is a world-famous tourist attraction[17] because of the canals[18] that form many of its "streets." Boats called "gondolas" take people from one area of the city to another. The commercial spirit[19] of Venice lives on today in the busy Rialto market. There, tourists can find all sorts of[20] goods[21] on sale[22].

10. **surviving** [sɚ`vaɪvɪŋ] (a.) 倖存的
11. **form** [fɔːrm] (v.) 形成；成立
12. **republic** [rɪ`pʌblɪk] (n.) 共和政體
13. **commerce** [`kɑːmɜːrs] (n.) 商業
14. **develop** [dɪ`vɛləp] (v.) 發展；開發
15. **commercial** [kə`mɜːrʃəl] (a.) 商業的
16. **hub** [hʌb] (n.) 輪軸；中樞；中心

17. **tourist attraction** 觀光勝地
18. **canal** [kə`næl] (n.) 運河
19. **spirit** [`spɪrɪt] (n.) 精神
20. **all sorts of** 各種各樣的
21. **goods** [gʊdz] (n.) 貨物；商品
22. **on sale** 廉價出售

Chapter Two

The Loan

🎧 9

Meanwhile[1], in Venice, Antonio and Bassanio found Shylock. He was at the Rialto, as usual[2].

"Shylock, I have a request[3] for you," said Antonio. "I'd like you to loan[4] three thousand ducats[5] to my best friend, Bassanio. I will sign the contract. I'll happily pay you back in a few days[6]. I'll have plenty of[7] money when my ships arrive."

1. **meanwhile** [ˋmiːnwaɪl] (adv.) 與此同時
2. **as usual** 如同往常；照舊
3. **request** [rɪˋkwɛst] (n.) 請求
4. **loan** [loʊn] (v.) 借貸
5. **ducat** [ˋdʌkət] (n.) 中古世紀 歐洲的「達卡」金幣或銀幣
6. **in a few days** 在數日內
7. **plenty of** 許多的
8. **grumble** [ˋgrʌmbl] (v.) 抱怨
9. **do business with sb** 跟某人做生意
10. **not ever** 決不 (= never)
11. **Very well.** 好吧（置於句首）

"I have an idea," said Bassanio. "Why don't we go out to dinner? We can talk more about this loan."

"I never eat with Christians," grumbled[8] Shylock. "I may lend them money or do business with[9] them. But I don't eat with them. Not ever[10]!"

"Very well[11]," said Bassanio. "Why don't you just lend me the money, then? You know that Antonio will pay you back."

🎧 10

As Shylock listened to Antonio and Bassanio, he became angrier and angrier. How foolish these two men were! They knew how much he hated them. And yet[1] they were asking[2] him for a loan! He was determined to[3] make Antonio pay dearly[4].

"Shylock!" yelled Antonio. "Are you going to lend us the money or not? Answer me!"

Shylock answered him slowly. "Do you remember all of those times that you insulted[5] me in a loud voice[6] that everyone could hear? You once[7] spat[8] on me and called[9] me a dog. And now you want to borrow money from me, a dog!"

1. **and yet** 然而
2. **ask sb for** 要求某人……
3. **be determined to** 決心要
4. **dearly** [ˋdɪrli] (adv.) 付出巨大代價地
5. **insult** [ɪnˋsʌlt] (v.) 侮辱
6. **in a loud voice** 大聲
7. **once** [wʌns] (adv.) 曾經
8. **spit** [spɪt] (v.) 吐口水 (spit-spat-spat)
9. **call sb** 罵某人是……
10. **ask sb a favor** 請求某人的幫忙（favor 幫忙）
11. **be willing to** 願意
12. **on time** 準時地

"Look! I'm not asking you a favor[10]. You can charge me any interest you want. I don't mind. My ships will arrive any day now."

"Alright, Antonio. I'm willing to[11] lend you the money. I won't even charge you any interest. Just pay me back the loan on time[12]."

37

🎧 11

Antonio couldn't believe his ears. "What did you say?"

"I said you didn't know me. You always call me a cheapskate[1], but I am not. I will help you. I won't even charge you a single ducat. However, there's something I'm worried about. What if you don't pay me back?"

"Don't worry, Shylock. I'll pay you back."
"Well, I need some kind of a guarantee[2], don't I? Three thousand ducats is a lot of money. If you don't pay me back on time, I want a pound of[3] flesh[4]. I'll take a pound of flesh from any part of your body."

Antonio didn't like what Shylock proposed[5]. "No. I'd rather pay some interest if I'm late on[6] the payment."

1. **cheapskate** [ˋtʃiːpskeɪt] (n.) 小氣鬼
2. **guarantee** [ˌgærənˋtiː] (n.) 保證；打包票
3. **a pond of** 一磅重的
4. **flesh** [flɛʃ] (n.) （人類或動物的）肉
5. **propose** [prəˋpouz] (v.) 提議；提出（計畫）
6. **be late on** 在某方面遲了
7. **fellow** [ˋfelou] (n.) 同行的
8. **besides** [bɪˋsaɪdz] (adv.) 何況
9. **lawyer** [ˋlɑːjər] (n.) 律師
10. **judge** [dʒʌdʒ] (n.) 法官

"I'm afraid that's no good," said Shylock as
he laughed.

"Do you think I'd take money from a
fellow[7] moneylender? Besides[8], this contract
is only a joke! Do you think that any lawyer[9]
or judge[10] would believe me? Would they
really believe that I want a pound of your
flesh? You don't have to worry about
anything! It's my way of saying the bad
feelings of the past between us are finished."

✓ Check Up **What is the guarantee that Shylock wants?**

[a] Contract paper.　　[b] A pound of flesh.　　[c] Nothing.

Antonio pulled Bassanio aside[1] and spoke to him secretly[2].

"I don't want to do business with this man. He's evil[3]. And I know that he'd take the pound of flesh from me if he could. Let's see if somebody else will lend us the money."

But Bassanio had other ideas. "Who else in Venice can lend me this much money? Besides, this man is crazy. Don't worry about the guarantee. Nobody would make you pay a pound of flesh! Everyone will think he's nuts[4]!"

So, Antonio agreed to the conditions of the loan. The three men went to a lawyer and signed an agreement[5].

1. **pull sb aside** 把人拉到一旁
   aside 旁邊；一旁
2. **secretly** [`si:krətli] (adv.)
   秘密地
3. **evil** [`i:vəl] (a.) 邪惡的
4. **nuts** [nʌts] (a.) 瘋的
5. **agreement** [ə`gri:mənt] (n.)
   協議（書）
6. **for so long** 很久了
7. **because of + N./Ving**
   因為⋯⋯緣故

A strange smile came over Shylock's face. In fact, Shylock wanted to take a pound of flesh from Antonio. He'd hated Antonio for so long[6]. And he lost a lot of money because of[7] this generous moneylender.

One Point Lesson

● And I know that he'**d** take the pound of flesh from me if he could.

而且我知道，要是他辦得到，他一定會從我身上取下一磅肉。

---

would：① 將會（祈使句）
② 想要、願意（過去的主張、意志），大概會、會（假設語句）。

🅔🅖 She **would** not listen to my advice.

她不肯（想要）聽我的勸告。

13

Bassanio took the money that Antonio had borrowed although he had a bad feeling about[1] the loan contract.

He bought many gifts and clothes that he needed to propose to Portia. He then loaded[2] the gifts into a carriage[3]. He and his servant, Gratiano, went to Portia's house with the carriage.

When Bassanio arrived, Portia was delighted[4]. She had hoped that he would return[5] for her. She was in love with him.

1. **have a bad feeling about sth** 對某事有不祥之感
2. **load** [loud] (v.) 將東西裝上車或船
3. **carriage** [ˋkerɪdʒ] (n.) 四輪馬車
4. **delighted** [dɪˋlaɪtɪd] (a.) 高興的；歡喜的
5. **return** [rɪˋtɜːrn] (v.) 返回
6. **awful** [ˋɔːfəl] (a.) 可怕的
7. **broke** [brouk] (a.) 破產的
8. **sth means nothing to sb** 某事對某人來說毫無意義
9. **ever after** 從此以後

"Portia, I'm so happy to see you again,"
said Bassanio. "But I have something awful[6]
to tell you. I'm broke[7]. I have no money."

"Bassanio! Don't worry about that! I have
all of the money we need. Money means
nothing to me[8]. The only thing you have to
worry about is choosing the right
box. Then, we can live
happily ever after[9]."

Portia told
Bassanio about
her father's
contract.

One Point Lesson

● She **had hoped** that he would return for her.
她曾希望他會回來找她。

had + 過去分詞：過去完成式，表示在過去的某個時間點
上，所述的事情已經發生了。此句型多用於敘述故事，或
以前的事。

● The train **had already left** when I got to the station.
我到達車站時，火車已經開走了。

43

14

"Alright. I'll go choose the box now."

Portia started to worry. What if he chose the wrong box?

"Don't choose today. I have a bad feeling. I want you to wait."

"Wait! But the sooner I choose, the sooner[1] I can marry you. I can't wait any longer[2]."

"Then let me hire[3] a musician[4]. Maybe the music will help you think more clearly."

A little while later[5], a musician came.
He began to play soothing[6] music. Bassanio
slowly walked over to the golden chest.
He looked at it carefully.

"This can't be it," he said to himself.
"It's too obvious[7]. Everyone would choose the
golden one first. I think Portia's father
wanted to separate[8] the wise men from the
fools."

Then, he walked over to the silver chest.
"If men didn't choose the golden chest, then
they would choose this one. That's obvious,
as well."

1. **the sooner . . ., the sooner
. . .** 愈早……就愈早……
2. **not . . . any longer** 再也不
= no longer
3. **hire** [haɪr] (v.) 聘用
4. **musician** [mjuːˋzɪʃən] (n.)
樂師

5. **a little while later**
過了一會兒
6. **soothing** [ˋsuːðɪŋ] (a.)
安撫的；舒緩的
7. **obvious** [ˋɑːbvɪəs] (a.)
顯而易見的
8. **separate A from B**
區別 A 與 B

> **One Point Lesson**
>
> Then let me hire a musician.
> 那麼讓我僱請一位樂師來。
>
> **let + 受詞 + 原形動詞**：祈使句句型，讓某人做某件事。
>
> I'll let you know when he comes.
> 他來的時候我會讓你知道。

15

Bassanio's eyes settled on[1] the lead chest.

"This is the least obvious choice. I don't think anyone else would choose this one."

He opened the box. He gasped[2]. He couldn't believe his eyes! In the box was a small picture of Portia. Bassanio could now marry her!
He was so happy that he couldn't even speak.

1. **settle on** 棲息在
2. **gasp** [gæsp] (v.) 倒抽氣
3. **put one's arms around sb**
   仲臂環抱某人
4. **proposal** [prəˋpouzəl] (n.)
   求婚

5. **put on** 戴上；穿上
6. **take off** 脫下；取下
7. **be married to sb**
   與某人結婚
8. **wear a ring** 戴戒指
9. **swear** [swer] (v.) 發誓
   (swear-swore-sworn)

Portia put her arms around[3] him and said, "Oh, Bassanio! I'm the luckiest woman in the world. Yesterday, I was just a girl with a lot of money. Today, I'll be a wife. Please, take this ring and show me you will accept my proposal[4]. Put it on[5] and promise me that you'll never take it off[6]."

"I am lucky, too," said Bassanio. "Yesterday, I was poor and lonely. Today, I will be married to[7] the most beautiful woman in the world. I promise that I'll wear[8] this ring forever. Until I die! I swear[9]!"

Check Up **Why did he choose the lead box?**
a Because nobody would choose it.
b Because he knew Portia loved lead.
c Because Portia told him that was the right one.

Ans: a

47

16

It was a very happy moment[1]. Gratiano felt that it was a good time to[2] ask Bassanio something.

"Since you're getting married[3], I'd like to[4] get married, too."

"Well, that's wonderful," said Bassanio. "But who are you going to marry?"

"I want to marry Nerissa."

Bassanio and Portia were very surprised.

"I didn't know you wanted to get married, Nerissa," cried Portia. "This is a great day!"

That evening the couples[5] got married. Bassanio and Gratiano wore golden rings that they promised never to take off. They were the happiest men in the world.

1. **moment** [ˋmoumənt] (n.) 時刻
2. **it is a good time to** 這是做……的好時機
3. **get married** 結婚
4. **would like to** 想要……
5. **couple** [ˋkʌpl] (n.) 一對；夫婦

One Point Lesson

◆ Bassanio and Portia were very surprised.
巴薩尼奧和波蒂亞感到非常驚喜。

驚喜（意外）都是外界情況或事物所引發的感受，所以是被動地獲得，故而用過去分詞表示。當主動造成驚喜（意外）時，則用現在分詞表示：It's a surprising gift.

e.g. I am pleased with the result.
這結果使我滿意（我滿意這結果）。

A True or False

T F **1** Shylock went out to dinner with Antonio.

T F **2** Shylock did not charge Antonio any interest.

T F **3** There was a small picture of Portia in the golden chest.

T F **4** Gratiano and Nerissa wanted to get married.

T F **5** Bassanio promised that he would wear his wedding ring forever.

B Complete the sentences with antonyms of the words underlined.

1 Bassanio _____ three thousand ducats from Shylock.

(↔ lent)

2 Shylock _____ Antonio for so long.

(↔ liked)

3 Money means _____ to Portia.

(↔ everything)

4 Portia worried that Antonio would choose the _____ box.

(↔ right)

C Choose the best answers to the questions.

1 What kind of guarantee did Shylock want?

(a) He wanted a lot for interest.

(b) He wanted a pound of flesh from Antonio's body.

(c) He just wanted Antonio to pay back on time.

2 Why did Bassanio feel that he was lucky?

(a) Because he had three thousand ducats.

(b) Because he had a lot of money.

(c) Because he was going to marry the most beautiful woman in the world.

D Rewrite the sentences according to the examples above.

They are foolish. ⇨ *How foolish* they are!

It is a pretty doll. ⇨ *What a pretty doll* it is!

1 She is beautiful. ⇨ _____

2 He is a handsome man. ⇨ _____

3 They have a big house. ⇨ _____

4 The trees are tall. ⇨ _____

Chapter Three

The Debt

A few days later, a messenger[1] arrived at Portia and Bassanio's house. Bassanio received the letter and opened it. It read:

Dear Bassanio,

My ships have all sunk[2]. I am in big trouble. Shylock wants to take a pound of flesh from me. Everyone has tried to talk him out of[3] it. Even the Duke[4] of Venice has tried. But no one has had any success.
I am going to die. Please come to my trial[5] and execution[6]. I want to see you once more. Come quickly. I don't have much time.

Your Friend,
Antonio

As Bassanio read the note[7], his face turned white. He had to sit down. His hands trembled[8].

1. **messenger** [`mesɪndʒər] (n.) 信差
2. **sink** [sɪŋk] (v.) 沉 (sink-sank-sunk)
3. **talk sb out of** 勸某人打消某想法或做法
4. **duke** [du:k] (n.) 公爵
5. **trial** [`traɪəl] (n.) 審判
6. **execution** [`eksɪkju:t] (n.) 行刑
7. **note** [nout] (n.) 短箋
8. **tremble** [`trembl] (v.) 顫抖

Portia ran to him. "What is it? What's wrong? Please! Answer me!"

"Oh! My poor friend Antonio! He's going to die! Portia, listen to me carefully. I am not only a poor man. I am a debtor[1] as well."

Bassanio told her all about the money and the pound of flesh.

A chill[2] ran through[3] Portia's body. She couldn't believe that a man wanted to cut[4] a pound of flesh from someone.

"Bassanio, go to your friend right away," she said. "You are my husband now. My money is your money. You must pay back Antonio's debt. I'll give you two times[5] the original[6] loan. Go quickly before Antonio is killed."

1. **debtor** [ˋdetər] (n.) 債務人
2. **chill** [tʃɪl] (n.) 寒意
3. **run through** 貫穿；竄流
4. **cut** [kʌt] (v.) 切割
5. **two times** 兩倍
6. **original** [əˋrɪdʒɪnəl] (a.) 原本的；最初的
7. **leave for** 動身前往
8. **prison** [ˋprɪzən] (n.) 監牢
9. **hug** [hʌg] (v.) 擁抱 (hug-hugged-hugged)
10. **go free** 自由；被釋放
11. **after all** 畢竟；終究

Bassanio put a lot of money in a bag and left for[7] Venice. He found Antonio in prison[8]. When he saw his friend, Antonio ran to him and hugged[9] him. Antonio looked small and weak.

"My dear friend," said Bassanio. "I'll go to Shylock today and pay back the money. I'm sure he'll take it and then you can go free[10]. After all[11], he is very greedy. He won't say 'no' to money."

19

"Dear Bassanio," said Antonio. "You are too kind. But I think it's too late. Shylock wants a pound of flesh from me. According to[1] the loan agreement, that's what I owe him. You won't be able to talk him out of it."

"He's never refused[2] money before."
"This time it's different. He hates me so much that he wants to kill me. And to make matters worse[3], Jessica ran away from[4] home."

"Jessica? Do you mean Shylock's daughter?"
"That's right. She married the young man who was living in your parents' house. The Christian boy. She is going to give up[5] her religion and become a Christian. And when she ran away from home, she stole[6] a gem[7] from Shylock, too."

1. **according to** 依照
2. **refuse** [rɪˋfjuːz] (v.) 拒絕
3. **to make matters worse** 使事情更糟
4. **run away from** 逃離
5. **give up** 放棄；捨棄
6. **steal** [stiːl] (v.) 偷竊 (steal-stole-stolen)
7. **gem** [dʒem] (n.) 寶石
8. **have nothing to do with** 與……無關
9. **mad** [mæd] (a.) 瘋狂的；很生氣的
10. **cut sb out of** 把某人從……中除名
11. **will** [wɪl] (n.) 遺囑

"Oh! That's terrible," said Bassanio.

"He probably thinks that I made her marry the Christian. But I have nothing to do with[8] it.

I swear! He's really mad[9]! He cut Jessica out of[10] his will[11]. And, for the past few days, Shylock's been talking about me. He's told everyone that he's going to kill me."

20

"Don't worry about that," said Bassanio. "I'll talk to Shylock. I'll make him change his mind[1]. I'll do whatever[2] I need to."

Bassanio went out of the prison and found Shylock.

"Please, I beg[3] you. Please spare[4] Antonio's life.

Please, please release[5] him from prison. Here's six thousand ducats. That's twice[6] the amount we borrowed in the first place[7]."

Bassanio begged on his hands and knees[8],

1. **change one's mind** 改變心意
2. **whatever** [wɑːtˋevər] (pron.)
   無論什麼
3. **beg** [beg] (v.) 央求；乞求
   (beg-begged-begged)
4. **spare one's life** 饒某人的命
5. **release** [rɪˋliːze] (v.) 釋放
6. **twice** [twaɪs] (adv.) 兩倍
   = two times
7. **in the first place** 當初
8. **on one's hands and knees**
   匍匐在地；伏跪
9. **name one's/the price** 開價
10. **realize** [ˋriːlaɪz] (v.) 覺察
11. **court** [kɔːrt] (n.) 法庭
    go to court 上法庭

"No. I want a pound of flesh. He owes me that."

"I'll give you nine thousand ducats. Just let him live!"

"No."

"Name your price[9]. I'll pay you anything."

"I want a pound of flesh."

Bassanio realized[10] that Shylock would not change his mind. There was only one thing that he could do. He had to go to court[11].

◦ There was only one thing **that** he could do.
他能做的只有一件事。

---

that：在這裡作關係代名詞，代表他唯一能做的那件事。
the only 可換為 the first, the last, the very thing。

e.g. She is the first girl **that** I saw.
她是我瞧見的第一個女孩。

21

At that time, everyone of Venice was talking about the problem. Everyone felt sorry for[1] Antonio. He had only wanted to help a friend. And everyone hated Shylock. He was such an evil man. More than being evil, however, he was angry.

He was angry with Antonio. Antonio had always spoken roughly[2] to him at the Rialto. He had cursed[3] Shylock for being a Jew. He had yelled at him for being a mean[4] and greedy businessman.

Shylock was also very angry about his daughter. His whole world was a dark and nasty[5] place. And he had nothing but[6] hatred in his heart for these two Christians, Antonio and Bassanio.

A date was set[7] for the trial. It was a very important trial. Even the Duke of Venice was involved[8]. He would be the judge.

1. **feel sorry for sb**
   為某人感到難過
2. **roughly** [ˋrʌfli] (adv.)
   粗魯無禮地
3. **curse** [kɜːrs] (v.) 咒罵
4. **mean** [miːn] (a.)
   惡毒的；吝嗇的
5. **nasty** [ˋnæsti] (a.)
   骯髒不潔的；令人厭惡的
6. **nothing but** 只有……
7. **be set** 訂定；確定
8. **be involved** 被捲入

22

Meanwhile, in Belmont, Portia heard about[1] the trial. She decided that she had to help poor Antonio. She could not rely on[2] fate[3] to change the course[4] of events[5].

Portia wrote a letter to her cousin, Bellario. He was a well-known[6] lawyer. She asked for his opinion[7] about Antonio's case[8]. She also asked him to lend her the clothes that he wore in court.

1. **heard about sth** 得知某事
2. **rely on** 指望
3. **fate** [feɪt] (n.) 命運
4. **course** [kɔːrs] (n.)
   發展；前進路線
5. **event** [ɪ`vent] (n.) 事情
6. **well-known** [`wel`noʊn] (a.)
   知名的
7. **opinion** [ə`pɪnjən] (n.)
   見解；看法

8. **case** [keɪs] (n.) 案件
9. **instructions** [ɪn`strʌkʃən] (n.)
   指示；吩咐的事項
10. **defend** [dɪ`fend] (v.) 辯護
11. **two sets of clothes** 兩套衣服
12. **dress in** 穿著……
13. **Venetian** [və`niːʃən] (n.)
    威尼斯人

A few days later,
a letter and a box
arrived in Belmont.
The letter had
instructions[9] for
defending[10] Antonio.
In the box were two sets
of clothes[11] that Bellario wore in court.

Portia dressed in[12] one set. She made
Nerissa wear the other set. Then they left for
Venice.

Portia and Nerissa went to the Grand
Court House of Venice. There, they waited for
the trial to begin. On the day of trial, it
seemed like every Venetian[13] came to the
court. Everyone wanted to know what would
happen to Antonio.

One Point Lesson

◆ **In the box** were two sets of clothes that Bellario
wore in court.
箱子裡，是兩套貝拉里奧在法庭上穿的衣服。

原句的完整式是：「There were two sets of clothes
that Bellario wore in court in the box.」此處 there 就
是 in the box（在箱子裡），可以直接用 in the box 取代
there，故而省略了。

● **Here** comes David! 大衛來了！

A True or False.

T F **1** Shylock accepted nine thousand ducats instead of Antonio's flesh.

T F **2** Shylock's daughter married a Christian.

T F **3** Everyone in Venice felt sorry for Antonio.

T F **4** Portia relied on fate to change the course of events.

T F **5** Bellario was a well-known judge.

B Rearrange the following sentences in chronological order.

1 Bassanio told Portia about the pound of flesh.

2 Bassanio put a lot of money in a bag and left for Venice.

3 Bassanio begged Shylock to release Antonio from prison.

4 Bassanio received a letter from Antonio.

5 Bassanio found Antonio in prison.

_____ ⇨ _____ ⇨ _____ ⇨ _____ ⇨ _____

C Choose the best answer to each question.

1 Why couldn't Antonio pay Shylock back?

(a) Because his ships have all sunk.

(b) Because he was in prison.

(c) Because Bassanio didn't lend him money.

2 What was in the box that Bellario sent to Portia?

(a) A gem that he stole from Shylock.

(b) A book that he wrote.

(c) Two sets of clothes that he wore in court.

D Fill in the blanks with the given words.

cursed   instructions   opinion   evil   change

1 Everyone hated Shylock. He was an _____ man.

2 Bassanio realized that Shylock would not _____ his mind.

3 Antonio had _____ Shylock for being a Jew.

4 Portia asked for Bellario's _____ about Antonio's case.

5 The letter from Bellario had _____ for defending Antonio.

Shylock
— Is he really such a bad character?

Some people have criticized[1] The Merchant of Venice for showing Jewish people in a bad way. However, it is also argued[2] that Shakespeare was just using historical facts to create[3] his characters[4].

1. **criticize** [ˋkrɪtɪsaɪz] (v.) 批評；抨擊
2. **argue** [ˋɑrgjuː] (v.)
   爭論；提出理由來主張
3. **create** [kriˋeɪt] (v.) 創造
4. **character** [ˋkerɪtər] (n.) 人物；角色

Venice at the time of his play was a commercial Christian city. Young Christian men like Antonio and Bassanio could make fortunes[5] by investing[6] in ships that carried valuable[7] goods around the Mediterranean[8].

However, to make money, you need to have money. Christians thought it was "evil" to charge interest when they lent money. Therefore, Christians had no financial[9] reasons to lend money to others.

However, the Jewish religion did not have any rules against charging interest. And moneylending was sometimes the only way a Jew could support[10] himself and his family in the Christian world of commerce. So many Jews, like Shylock, made their business by lending money and earning interest. This is why many Christians thought that Jews were "greedy."

Shylock is seen as a greedy man. Unfortunately, this reflects[11] a common stereotype[12] of Jews in medieval[13] and modern times. So was he really such a bad character? What do you think?

5. **make a fortune** 致富；發財
6. **invest** [ɪn`vɛst] (v.) 投資；挹注
7. **valuable** [`væljʊbl] (a.) 貴重的
8. **the Mediterranean** 地中海 9. **financial** [faɪ`nænʃəl] (v.) 金融的；財務的
10. **support** [sə`pɔrt] (v.) 扶養；養活
11. **reflect** [rɪ`flɛkt] (v.) 反映
12. **stereotype** [`stɛriətaɪp] (n.) 刻板印象
13. **medieval** [ˌmɛdɪ`iːvəl] (a.) 中古時期

The Trial

When the trial began, Portia gave the Duke of Venice a letter. The letter was from Bellario. It said that he could not be Antonio's lawyer because he was sick.

Bellario wrote that Balthasar would be Antonio's lawyer instead[1]. Balthasar was actually Portia in disguise[2]. The Duke didn't mind that Balthasar would represent[3] Antonio. He did wonder, however, if Balthasar was experienced[4] enough. "He" looked very young.

---

1. **instead** [ɪn`sted] (adv.)
   作為替代
2. **in disguise** 喬裝地
3. **represent** [ˌreprɪ`zent] (v.)
   代表
4. **experienced** [ɪk`spɪriənst]
   (a.) 有經驗的
5. **huge** [hjuːdʒ] (a.) 巨大的

6. **courtroom** [`kɔːrtruːm] (n.)
   法庭
7. **begging** [`begɪŋ] (a.)
   乞求的
8. **look over at**
   越過一段距離看；瞭望
9. **either**
   也不，用於否定句

Portia looked around the huge[5] courtroom[6]. Shylock seemed to be enjoying his day in court. Antonio looked at her with begging[7] eyes. Portia then looked over at[8] her husband. Bassanio didn't realize that Balthasar was actually his wife, either[9].

🎧24

As the trial began, the room grew quiet[1]. Portia spoke to Shylock first.

"Sir. According to the agreement, you can take a pound of flesh from Antonio. There's no question about that[2]. But I want to remind[3] you of another choice. Of a more noble[4] choice.

1. **grow + adj.** 變得……
2. **There's no question about that.** 那是毫無問題的。
3. **remind sb of sth** 提醒某人某事
4. **noble** [`noʊbl] (a.) 高貴的
5. **merciful** [`mɜːrsɪfəl] (a.) 慈悲的；仁慈的
6. **mercy** [`mɜːrsi] (n.) 慈悲
7. **heaven** [`hevən] (n.) 上蒼
8. **bless** [bles] (v.) 賜福；滋潤
9. **citizen** [`sɪtɪzən] (n.) 市民；國民；公民
10. **except for** 除了
11. **care about** 關心
12. **justice** [`dʒʌstɪs] (n.) 公正

You could choose to be merciful[5]. You may ask, 'What is mercy[6]?' Well, I'll tell you. Mercy is like the gentle rain. It falls from heaven[7]. It blesses[8] everyone. It blesses the person who gives mercy and the person who takes it. Mercy makes you feel like a king. You have all of the power in the world. You have the power to give Antonio his life. It is only through mercy that you can do this."

All of the citizens[9] in the courtroom agreed with Portia. Everyone except for[10] Shylock.

"I don't care about[11] mercy! I only want justice[12]!" he yelled.

Check Up Shylock wants _____ instead of _____.

a justice, mercy
b mercy, power
c power, justice

25

"Well, why don't you just allow[1] Antonio to pay you back?"

"It's too late for that now. I don't want money. I want my pound of flesh. Read the contract. It says that I can take the pound of flesh. And it says that I can take it from the place nearest to his heart."

"Antonio, you must get ready to[2] die, then," said Portia. Everyone in the crowd[3] gasped. They couldn't believe what they were hearing.

1. **allow sb to** 允許某人……
2. **get ready to** 做好……準備
3. **crowd** [kraʊd] (n.) 群眾
4. **pleading** [ˈpliːdɪŋ] (a.) 請求的；懇求的
5. **in a . . . voice** 用……聲音
6. **tear up** 撕掉 (tear-tore-torn)
7. **sharpen** [ˈʃɑːrpən] (v.) 使鋒利
8. **can't wait to** 迫不及待
9. **cut into** （用刀）切入……

"Shylock," said Portia in a pleading[4] voice[5]. "please, take this money and let me tear up[6] the loan contract."

Shylock said, "I will never change my mind. Not for any reason."

He began sharpening[7] his long knife. He couldn't wait to[8] cut into[9] Antonio.

Check Up **Shylock wants to do as the contract _____.**

a says   b does   c sees

Ans: a

26

Portia turned to[1] Antonio. "Do you have anything to say before you die?"

"No," said Antonio. "I am ready to[2] die."

Then he turned to Bassanio. "Goodbye, my friend. Don't blame[3] yourself for my death."

Bassanio was crying. "Oh, Antonio. I would do anything to save your life. But there's nothing I can do. I'm so sorry. You are the best friend in the world."

"Enough of this," yelled Shylock. "Let's get on with[4] it. I want my pound of flesh."

Portia asked the Duke, "Is the scale[5] ready?" The Duke nodded[6]. "Is the doctor here?"

"What doctor?" asked Shylock.

"There should be a doctor here. Antonio shouldn't bleed to death[7]."

But, of course, Shylock wanted him to bleed to death.

"The contract says nothing about a doctor."

"But surely we need a doctor here. It's the only decent[8] thing to do!"

1. **turn to sb** 轉向某人
2. **be ready to** 準備好去做
3. **blame sb for sth**
   為某事責怪某人
4. **get on with**
   （中斷後）繼續進行

5. **scale** [skeɪl] (n.) 磅秤
6. **nod** [nɑːd] (v.) 點頭；頷首
   (nod-nodded-nodded)
7. **bleed to death** 流血至死
   (bleed-bled-bled)
8. **decent** [`diːsənt] (a.) 正當的

One Point Lesson

● Do you have **anything to say** before you die?
你有什麼遺言？

anything, something, nothing：意思雖各有不同，但是
用在此句中，只有語氣的差異，意思相仿。

e.g. Is there **anything** cold? 有沒有什麼冷飲啊？

27

"The contract says nothing about a doctor," Shylock repeated.

"Alright," said Portia. "A pound of flesh is yours. The law allows it. The court awards[1] it."

Shylock was very happy that he could finally kill his enemy. He was very pleased with[2] the young lawyer.

"You are such a good lawyer," he said. "You understand justice."

Shylock picked up his sharp knife. It was bright and shiny[3]. The moneylender had an evil look[4] in his eyes.

1. **award** [əˋwɔːrd] (v.) 裁定（賠償金等）給……
2. **be pleased with sb** 對某人感到滿意
3. **shiny** [ˋʃaɪni] (a.) 閃亮的
4. **look** [lʊk] (n.) 眼神
5. **a drop of** 一滴
6. **break the law** 觸犯法律

"Come here," he said to Antonio.

"Just a minute," said Portia. "There is another thing I need to tell you. This contract doesn't give you a drop of[5] blood. If Antonio loses a drop of blood, you will break the law[6]. The City of Venice will take all of your money and land. Do you understand?"

The Merchant of Venice

Shylock didn't know what to say[1].
Everything had changed. He couldn't possibly[2]
get his revenge[3] now. His face turned red with
anger.

Everyone was very impressed with[4] this
young lawyer. "Balthasar" used the terms[5] of
the contract to save Antonio. There was no
mention[6] of blood in the contract. Shylock
could not take any blood. Therefore, he
couldn't take any flesh, either.

The people in the courtroom clapped[7] their
hands. "Hooray for Balthasar[8]!"

Shylock slammed[9] his fist[10] against the
table.

"Well, where's my money, then? If I can't
have my pound of flesh, I want my money."

"Here it is." Bassanio happily threw him a
bag with three thousand ducats inside.
Shylock began to walk away.

1. **what to say** 要說什麼
2. **possibly** [`pɑːsəbli] (adv.)
   說不定；可能地
3. **get one's revenge** 報復得逞
4. **be impressed with**
   對……感到佩服
5. **terms** [tɜːrmz] (n.) 契約條款
6. **mention** [`menʃən] (n.) 提及
7. **clap one's hands** 拍手
8. **hooray for sb** 為某人歡呼
9. **slam** [slæm] (v.) 重擊
10. **fist** [fɪst] (n.) 拳頭

"Not so fast," said Portia. "You tried to murder[1] someone. By law[2], you must give all of your money to the City of Venice. You could also be killed. You are at the mercy of[3] the Duke of Venice. Get down on your hands and knees[4]. Beg him for[5] forgiveness[6]."

"No," said the Duke. "I don't think anyone should have to beg for their life. It isn't right. I must make an important decision, and I must think about it carefully.

1. **murder** [`mɜrdər] (v.) 殺人
2. **by law** 依法
3. **at the mercy of** 聽憑……處置
4. **get down on one's knees** 跪下
5. **beg sb for sth** 向某人懇求某事
6. **forgiveness** [fər`gɪvnəs] (n.) 原諒；寬恕
7. **throw** [θroʊ] (n.) 扔；丟 (throw-threw-thrown)
8. **jail** [dʒeɪl] (n.) 監牢
9. **punishment** [`pʌnɪʃmənt] (n.) 懲罰；懲處
10. **courthouse** [`kɔːrthaʊs] (n.) 法院大樓

I want Shylock thrown[7] in jail[8] tonight. Tomorrow I will tell you what his punishment[9] will be."

Everyone left the courthouse[10] that afternoon. They walked through the streets talking about the trial. No one could remember a more unusual day.

One Point Lesson

◊ They walked through the streets **talking about the trial**. 他們穿過街道時，邊聊著審判。

此處的 talking about the trial（動名詞子句）作副詞補語，用來形容 walk through the streets 時的情形。動名詞子句也可用作原因。【注意】前後子句主詞要相同才可用此句型。

e.g. After he finished his study, he went to movies.
他讀完書之後才去看電影。
Finishing his study, he went to movies.
（因為）讀完了書，他才去看電影。

A Who said which sentence? Match it.

1 You could choose to be merciful. • • a The Duke

2 Don't blame yourself for my death. • • b Shylock

3 The contract says nothing about a doctor. • • c Antonio

4 I don't think that anyone should have to beg for their life. • • d Balthasar

B True or False.

T F 1 Bassanio realized that Balthasar was his wife.

T F 2 Shylock wanted Antonio to bleed to death.

T F 3 Balthasar used the terms of the contract to save Antonio's life.

T F 4 Shylock must be thrown in jail forever.

C Fill in the blanks with the given word.

> break   represent   sharpening   blesses   murder

❶ The Duke didn't mind that Balthasar would _____ Antonio.

❷ Mercy _____ the person who gives it and the person who takes it.

❸ Shylock began _____ his long knife.

❹ If Antonio loses a drop of blood, you will _____ the law.

❺ You also could be killed. You have tried to _____ someone.

D Match the two parts to make reasonable whole sentences.

❶ The Duke wondered •   • **ⓐ** you can take a pound of flesh from Antonio

❷ According to the law •   • **ⓑ** and let me tear up the loan contract.

❸ You have the power •   • **ⓒ** to give Antonio his life.

❹ Take this money •   • **ⓓ** if Balthasar was experienced enough.

Chapter Five

🎧 30 The Sentence[1]

The next morning was gray and rainy. Shylock felt that it was the last day of his life. The atmosphere[2] of the courtroom was very gloomy[3]. The crowd hated Shylock, but nobody wanted him to be killed.

When the Duke walked in, everyone became very quiet.

"Most people understand mercy," said the Duke, at last[4]. "It seems that you, Shylock, don't understand it. I am a human being[5]. I understand mercy. And I understand the value[6] of a human life.

In the spirit of mercy, I forgive[7] you. I will spare your life. I must punish you, though[8]. If I don't, maybe other people will act[9] like you. You must give half of your money to Antonio, and the other half to the City of Venice."

✔ *Check Up* **What is the punishment on Shylock?**

a To be killed.

b To give all of his money to Antonio and the City of Venice.

c To beg forgiveness.

Ans: b

1. **sentence** [ˋsentəns] (n.)
   判刑
2. **atmosphere** [ˋætməsfɪr] (n.)
   氣氛；氛圍
3. **gloomy** [glu:mi] (a.)
   黯淡的；情緒低的
4. **at last** 終於

5. **human being** 人類；凡人
6. **value** [ˋvælju:] (n.) 價值
7. **forgive** [fərˋgɪv] (v.) 原諒
8. **though** [ðou] (adv.)
   然而（多用於句尾）
9. **act** [ækt] (v.) 行動；表現

85

31

Antonio was always a generous man. Even after all that had happened, he didn't change. He knew that Shylock's daughter, Jessica, was poor.

"I have a request[1] about the money," said Antonio.
"What is your request?" asked the Duke.

The court became quiet again. The crowd leaned[2] forward to hear.

"I want to give Shylock's money to his daughter. And I want him to put Jessica back in his will."

"I think this is a fair[3] request Shylock,
I order[4] you to give half of your money to Jessica.
And you must write her back into your will.
If you don't do this, I'll throw you in jail for the rest of your life."

---

1. **request** [rɪˋkwest] (n.) 請求
2. **lean** [liːn] (v.) 傾（身）
3. **fair** [fer] (a.) 公平的；公道的
4. **order sb to** 命令某人去做
5. **fail to** 未能
6. **get revenge on sb** 報復某人
7. **be set free** 被釋放 (set-set-set)
8. **pull out** 拔出；拉出

Shylock felt sick. He had failed to [5] get revenge on [6] Antonio. He had lost his money. He hated everyone.

"Fine. I'll do what you want. Just let me go now. I am not feeling well."

Shylock was set free [7]. He walked through the streets pulling out [8] his hair. He couldn't believe his luck!

32

"Sir," said the Duke to Portia. "I have never seen such a clever[1] lawyer in my life. I must admit[2] that I was worried at first[3] because you looked so young. If you're not too busy, please have dinner with me tonight. I'd love to[4] talk about the law with you."

Portia wanted to get home[5] before her husband. "I would love to, but I have another case that I must work on[6]. I'm sorry. I'm just too busy to[7] have dinner with you tonight."

"Oh, well. Another time, then."

The Duke turned to Antonio. "You should pay this lawyer well. You owe him an awful lot[8]."

1. clever [`klɛvɚ] (a.)
   聰明的；機敏的
2. admit [əd`mɪt] (v.) 坦承
   (admit-admitted-admitted)
3. at first 一開始；起初
4. would love to 很想要……
5. get home 到家
6. work on 研究；努力地工作
7. too . . . to . . .
   太……，以致於不……
8. an awful lot 極多
9. not . . . at all
   一點也不（沒有）
10. wedding ring 婚戒

"Please," said Bassanio to Portia. "take these three thousand ducats. That's how much we borrowed from Shylock in the first place."

"I don't want the money."

"I'll give you three thousand more, then."

"I don't want any money at all[9]," said Portia. "Instead, I want your wedding ring[10]."

• I have never seen such a clever lawyer in my life.
　我這輩子從未見過如此聰明的律師。

現在完成式（**have + 過去分詞**）：用來表示所述的事情，在現在這個時間點，已經發生了。此外，**ever** 是 **never** 的反義詞。

e.g. She is the most beautiful girl I have ever seen.
　她是我所見過最美的女孩。

e.g. I have never been to New York. 我從未到過紐約。

89

33

"My wedding ring? I'm sorry. This is the one thing in the world that I can't give you. I promised my wife that I would never take it off. I will find you the most expensive ring in Venice. I will buy it for you now. But I can't give you this ring. No way[1]!"

"I want your wedding ring, but I'm not going to beg. I see that you're too cheap[2] to give it to me."

Portia left the courtroom. She seemed angry. Actually, she was happy.

---

1. **No way!** 絕對不行！休想！
2. **cheap** [tʃi:p] (a.) 〔口〕〔美〕小氣的
3. **ashamed** [əˋʃeɪmd] (a.) 慚愧的

"Please, Bassanio. Give him the ring," said Antonio.

"I know your wife will be mad. But think about what this lawyer has done for us today. I owe him my life. Don't you think that's worth your wedding ring?"

Bassanio felt ashamed[3]. Antonio was right. He took off his ring and gave it to Gratiano.

"Go and find Balthasar. Give him this ring."

When Gratiano found Portia, he gave her the ring. Nerissa, who was with her, said, "You! Gratiano! You give me your ring, too."

Gratiano knew that he couldn't say 'no.' He gave her his ring.

One Point Lesson

◆ Nerissa, **who was with her**, said, "You! Gratiano! You give me your ring, too."
跟她在一起的娜麗莎說道:「你!葛提諾!你也把你的戒指給我。」

這個句型中,子句 who was with her 作形容詞補語用。

e.g. Brian, **his English teacher**, was yelling at him.
他的英文老師布萊恩正在對他吼叫。

🎧 34

When Portia and Nerissa were alone, they had a good laugh[1]. They decided to play a trick on[2] their husbands.

Bassanio and Gratiano returned to Belmont that evening. They found their wives waiting[3] for them. They kissed their wives. For a moment[4], everyone was very happy to be together again.

1. **have a good laugh** 大笑一番
2. **play a trick on sb** 捉弄某人
3. **find sb V-ing**
   發現某人正在……
4. **for a moment**
   一時之間;有一下子
5. **scream** [skri:m] (v.) 尖叫
6. **as payment** 作為報償
7. **darling** [`dɑːrlɪŋ] (n.) 親愛的
8. **guilty** [`gɪlti] (a.) 內疚的

Then, the women started yelling at them.

"Where's your wedding ring?" cried Portia.

"You gave our wedding rings to other women," screamed[5] Nerissa.

"Please believe us," said Bassanio. "We gave our rings to two young lawyers. The lawyers saved the life of my best friend. They said that they wanted our wedding rings as payment[6]. They wouldn't accept anything else. Please understand, darling[7]. They saved Antonio's life!"

Bassanio felt sad and guilty[8].

✓ *Check Up* **What was the trick the two women played?**

a They pretended to forgive their husbands.
b They pretended to doubt their husbands.
c They pretended to save their husbands.

Ans: b

"I suppose[1] that there is only one thing we can do," said Portia. Bassanio was afraid. Gratiano's knees[2] were shaking[3].

"We must give you your rings back."

Portia opened her hand. Nerissa opened hers as well. Bassanio and Gratiano couldn't believe their eyes! They were holding[4] their wedding rings!

1. **suppose** [sə`poʊz] (v.) 猜想
2. **knee** [niː] (n.) 膝蓋
3. **shake** [ʃeɪk] (v.) 搖晃；發抖 (shake-shook-shaken)
4. **hold** [hoʊld] (v.) 握；抓 (hold-held-held)

Portia and Nerissa started to giggle[5].
Then they laughed harder and harder.
The men stood there with confused looks[6]
on their faces.

Finally, Portia began to tell their story.
Bassanio was amazed[7]. His wife was even
more wonderful than he had thought. She
was the cleverest woman in Italy. She saved
his best friend's life. He was overcome with[8]
happiness.

5. **giggle** [ˋgɪgl] (v.) 吃吃笑
6. **confused look**
   困惑的表情

7. **amazed** [əˋmeɪzd] (a.)
   吃驚的
8. **be overcome with**
   被……征服

As if[1] this surprise weren't enough, a messenger soon arrived with another. The man brought news that Antonio's ships had not sunk. They had safely arrived in Venice. The goods were ready for sale[2]. They couldn't have been happier.

That night, they all celebrated[3] under the beautiful Italian moon. They laughed thinking about the rings and the trick Portia and Nerissa had played on Bassanio and Gratiano.

1. **as if** 彷彿；宛如
2. **for sale** 待售
3. **celebrate** [`selɪbreɪt] (v.) 慶祝；祝賀
4. **lovingly** [`lʌvɪŋli] (v.) 疼愛地；深情地
5. **scary** [`skeri] (a.) 可怕的；使人驚恐的
6. **Absolutely not!** 絕對不是！才不是！

Bassanio looked lovingly[4] at his wife.

"What's the scariest[5] thing in the world?" he asked her.

"Owing a pound of flesh to a moneylender?" asked Portia.

"Absolutely not[6]! It's losing my wife's wedding ring."

Bassanio never took off his ring again.

A Rearrange the following sentences in chronological order.

❶ Bassanio gave Balthasar his wedding ring.

❷ Antonio wanted to give Shylock's money to his daughter.

❸ Shylock was set free, but he couldn't believe his luck.

❹ A messenger brought news that Antonio's ships had not sunk.

❺ Portia and Nerissa decided to play a trick on their husbands.

_____ ⇨ _____ ⇨ _____ ⇨ _____ ⇨ _____

B Fill in the blanks with the given words.

happiness   revenge   payment   value   atmosphere

❶ The _____ of the courtroom was very gloomy.

❷ I understand the _____ of a human life.

❸ Shylock failed to get _____ on Antonio.

❹ They wanted our wedding rings as _____.

❺ Bassanio was overcome with _____.

C Choose the right answer to each question.

1 Why did the Duke punish Shylock?

    (a) Because he didn't like him.

    (b) Because he didn't understand mercy.

    (c) Because if he didn't, maybe other people would act like him.

2 Why didn't Bassanio want to give the ring to Balthasar?

    (a) Because he wanted to give it to another woman.

    (b) Because he promised his wife that he would never take it off.

    (c) Because it was the most expensive ring in Venice.

D Fill in the person who said the words.

1 Fine. I'll do what you want. Just let me go now. _____

2 You should pay this lawyer well. You owe him an awful lot. _____

3 Think about what this lawyer has done for us today. _____

4 You! Gratiano! You give me your wedding ring, too. _____

Appendixes

1 Basic Grammar
2 Guide to Listening Comprehension
3 Listening Guide
4 Listening Comprehension

1　Basic Grammar

> 要增強英文閱讀理解能力，應練習找出英文的主結構。
> 要擁有良好的英語閱讀能力，首先要理解英文的段落結構。

「英文的閱讀理解從「分解文章」開始」

　　英文的文章是以「有意義的詞組」（指帶有意義的語句）所構成的。用（／）符號來區別各個意義語塊，請試著掌握其中的意義。

He knew　/　that she told a lie　/　at the party.　//
他知道　　　　她說了一個謊　　　　在派對上。

As she was walking　/　in the garden,　/　she smelled　/
她在散步時　　　　　　在花園裡　　　　她聞到

something wet.　//
某種濕濕的（氣味）。

一篇文章，要分成幾個有意義的詞組？

可放入（／）符號來區隔有意義詞組的地方，一般是在（1）「主詞＋動詞」之後；（2）and 和 but 等連接詞之前；（3）that、who 等關係代名詞之前；（4）副詞子句的前後，會用（／）符號來區隔。初學者可能在一篇文章中畫很多（／）符號，但隨著閱讀實力的提升，（／）會減少。時間一久，在不太複雜的文章中即使不畫（／）符號，也能一眼就理解整句的意義。

使用（／）符號來閱讀理解英語篇章
1. 能熟悉英文的句型和構造。
2. 可加速閱讀速度。

該方法對於需要邊聽理解的英文聽力也有很好的效果。
從現在開始，早日丟棄過去理解文章的習慣吧！

以直接閱讀理解的方式，重新閱讀《威尼斯商人》

從原文中摘錄一小段。以具有意義的詞組將文章做斷句區分，重新閱讀並做理解練習。

It happened / in a city / called Venice in Italy.
它發生　　／在一個城市／在義大利叫作威尼斯的。

This beautiful city rests / like a crown jewel / on the Adriatic Sea.
這個美麗的城市鑲嵌　／宛如一顆皇冠上的珠寶／在亞得里亞海上。

There lived a moneylender / named Shylock / in Venice.
那裡住著一個放貸者　　　／名叫夏洛克　　／在威尼斯城。

He earned a lot / by lending money to merchants.

他賺了很多錢　　／靠著借錢給商人。

Some people hated him / because he forced merchants / to repay him / in terrible ways.

有些人憎恨他　　　　　　／因為他迫使商人　　　　　　　　／償還他
　／用很悽慘的方式。

Others hated him / simply because he was Jewish.

其他人憎恨他　　／只因為他是猶太人。

Of all the merchants / who lived in Venice, / one hated Shylock / more than the others.

在所有商人當中　　　／住在威尼斯的　　　　／有一個憎恨夏洛克
／更勝其他人。

His name was Antonio. // Shylock hated Antonio / as well.

他的名字叫作安東尼奧　／夏洛克憎恨安東尼奧　　／也。

This was / because Antonio was a very generous moneylender.

這是　　／因為安東尼奧是一個非常慷慨的放貸者。

He lent money / to people in trouble / and often didn't charge / them interest. //

他借錢　　　　／給有困難的人　　／而且經常不收　　　　／他們
利息。

Shylock lost a lot of business / because of Antonio's generosity.

夏洛克失去了許多生意　　　／因為安東尼奧的寬宏大量。

More importantly, / Shylock hated Antonio / because he was a Christian. //

更重要地，　　　／夏洛克憎恨安東尼奧　　／因為他是基督徒。

And Antonio hated Shylock / because he was a Jew.

而安東尼奧憎恨夏洛克　　／因為他是猶太人。

In those days, / Jews and Christians didn't like / each other.
在那個年頭， / 猶太人和基督徒不喜歡 / 彼此。

They couldn't agree / about anything.
他們無法有一致的看法 / 對任何事情。

They couldn't understand / each other's religion or culture.
他們無法理解 / 彼此的宗教或文化。

Antonio and Shylock / often ran into / each other / at the Rialto.
安東尼奧和夏洛克 / 常常巧遇 / 彼此 / 在里艾爾托。

The Rialto was the business center / of Venice.
里艾爾托是商業中心 / 威尼斯的。

When the two met, / they would have arguments.
這兩個人見面時 / 就會起爭執。

Antonio would often yell / at Shylock / for the heartless way / of doing business.
安東尼奧經常大聲吼叫 / 對夏洛克 / 因為冷酷無情的方式 / 做生意的。

Shylock often thought / about ways / to get even with Antonio.
夏洛克常常思索 / 有關法子 / 報復安東尼奧。

Almost everyone in Venice / really liked Antonio.
在威尼斯幾乎人人 / 由衷喜歡安東尼奧。

They felt / that he was kind and honest.
他們覺得 / 他寬厚又誠實。

They knew / that he would help them / when they were in hard times.
他們知道 / 他會幫助他們 / 當他們在艱困時期。

Guide to Listening Comprehension

 When listening to the story, use some of the techniques shown below. If you take time to study some phonetic characteristics of English, listening will be easier.

Get in the flow of English.

English creates a rhythm formed by combinations of strong and weak stress intonations. Each word has its particular stress that combines with other words to form the overall pattern of stress or rhythm in a particular sentence.

When speaking and listening to English, it is essential to get in the flow of the rhythm of English. It takes a lot of practice to get used to such a rhythm. So, you need to start by identifying the stressed syllable in a word.

Listen for the strongly stressed words and phrases.

In English, key words and phrases that are essential to the meaning of a sentence are stressed louder. Therefore, pay attention to the words stressed with a higher pitch. When listening to an English recording for the first time, what matters most is to listen for a general understanding of what you hear. Do not try to hear every single word. Most of the unstressed words are articles or auxiliary verbs, which don't play an important role in the general context. At this level, you can ignore them.

Pay attention to liaisons.

In reading English, words are written with a space between them. There isn't such an obvious guide when it comes to listening to English. In oral English, there are many cases when the sounds of words are linked with adjacent words.

For instance, let's think about the phrase "take off," which can be used in "take off your clothes." "Take off your clothes" doesn't sound like [teɪk ɔːf] with each of the words completely and clearly separated from the others. Instead, it sounds as if almost all the words in context are slurred together, [ˈteɪkɔːf], for a more natural sound.

Shadow the voice of the native speaker.

Finally, you need to mimic the voice of the native speaker. Once you are sure you know how to pronounce all the words in a sentence, try to repeat them like an echo. Listen to the book again, but this time you should try a fun exercise while listening to the English.

This exercise is called "shadowing." The word "shadow" means a dark shade that is formed on a surface. When used as a verb, the word refers to the action of following someone or something like a shadow. In this exercise, pretend you are a parrot and try to shadow the voice of the native speaker.

Try to mimic the reader's voice by speaking at the same speed, with the same strong and weak stresses on words, and pausing or stopping at the same points.

Experts have already proven this technique to be effective. If you practice this shadowing exercise, your English speaking and listening skills will improve by leaps and bounds. While shadowing the native speaker, don't forget to pay attention to the meaning of each phrase and sentence.

Step 1 Listen to what you want to shadow many times. Start out by just trying to shadow a few words or a sentence.

 Step 2 Mimic the CD out loud. You can shadow everything the speaker says as if you are singing a round, or you also can speak simultaneously with the recorded voice of the native speaker.

 Step 3 As you practice more, try to shadow more. For instance, shadow a whole sentence or paragraph instead of just a few words.

3 Listening Guide

一開始若能聽清楚發音，之後就沒有聽力的負擔。先聽過摘錄的章節，之後再反覆聆聽括弧內單字的發音，並仔細閱讀各種發音的說明。以下都是以英語的典型發音為基礎，所做的簡易說明，即使這裡未提到的發音，也可以配合 CD 反覆聆聽，如此一來聽力必能更上層樓。

Chapter One page 14 🎧 37

I (**1**) (   ) story to tell. It is a story of love and hatred.
A story of giving and taking. A story of laughter and
tears. This story was told a long time ago.
But it (**2**) has as much meaning today as it did then.
It happened in a city called (**3**) (   ) (   ).

1 **have a:** 這兩個字連讀出時，a 發音極輕，聽的時候要仔細，說的時候要輕鬆。就像 and 這個字，例如 John and Mary，連讀時 and 幾乎只聽得到 n，a 和 d 都含在口中，發音非常含糊。多練習說它，聽力就會加強。

2 **still:** s 後面接續字母 p、t、k 時，因為 p、t、k 都是吐氣音，而 s 也是吐氣音，連在一起時發音無力，因此讀音會權宜地改為 b、d、g 的發音。也就是說，still 讀作 "sdill"，speak 讀作 "sbeak"，school 讀作 "sgool"。

3 **Venice in Italy:** 這三個字連讀時，in 的 i 是發很輕的 /ə/，有時甚至只聽得到 n。Italy 這個字，讀得快時，a 不發音，讀音為 /ɪtli/。

Meanwhile, in Venice, Antonio and Bassanio found Shylock. He was (❶) ( ) Rialto, as usual.
"Shylock, I have a (❷) ( ) you," said Antonio.
"I'd like you to loan three thousand ducats to my best friend, Bassanio. I will sign the contract. I'll happily pay you back in a few days. I'll have (❸) ( ) money when my ships arrive."

❶ **at the:** 連讀時，因為 t 立刻接上 the，兩者發音十分近似，因此 at 的 t 退居幕後，幾乎不發音，但聽或說時仍要意識到前面的字是 at。

❷ **request for:** 兩個字連讀時，因為 st 都是吐氣音，故而字尾 t 是含在嘴裡，幾乎聽不出來。如同 request to，前字的字尾 t 和後字的字首 t 合併，聽起來像是 reques to。此外，que 發音 /kwe/，把它想作ㄎㄨㄝ，就容易發音清楚了。

❸ **plenty of:** plenty 這個字在讀音時，t 的發音很輕，而因為它是吐氣音，有時甚至聽起來像似不發音，讀起來宛如 /pleni/，或近似 /plenli/。字母 nt 相連時，因為是兩個都是子音，t 幾乎只發頓音。

A few days (❶) a messenger (❷) (　) Portia and Bassanio's house. Bassanio received the letter and opened it. It read:

Dear Bassanio
My ships have all sunk. I am in big trouble. Shylock wants to take a pound of flesh from me. Everyone has (❸) (　) talk him out of it.

❶ **later:** 這個字裡的 t，讀得快時，美語讀音近似 l，英語讀音才會保持清楚的 t。如同 better，t 雖是吐氣音，但要把氣收住，不吐出去。

❷ **arrived at:** arrive 這個字，因為 v 是有聲音，故而過去式加上的 d 也是有聲音 d，而不讀作吐氣音 t。arrived at 連讀時，發音近似一個字 arrive-dat。

❸ **tried to:** 兩字連讀時，tried 雖然是過去式，但是因為 d 和字首 t 只有吐氣與不吐氣的差別，因此字尾 d 會退讓，讓字首 t 發音。也因此聽起來與現在式 try to 沒什麼分別。但是仔細聽就會發現，tried to 的 d 是含在口中，讀音時有些微頓音。

Chapter Four page 68 🎧40

When the trial began, Portia gave the Duke of Venice a letter. The letter was from Bellario. It said that he (❶) (　) be Antonio's lawyer because he (❷) (　).

❶ could not: 兩字連讀時，could 的字尾 d 是含在口中，聽起來只有些微頓音，而讓字首重音的 not 清楚地讀出。如同 couldn't，dn 連音時，d 也是含在口中輕頓。

❷ was sick: was 的字尾 s 讀音是 /z/，sick 的字首 s 讀音 /s/。兩字連讀時，雖然兩個 s 讀音不同，但仍是近似音，因此字尾 s 要讓位給字首 s，聽起來是合併為一個 s。

Chapter Five page 84 🎧 41

> The (❶) ( ) was gray and rainy. Shylock felt that it was the last day of his life. The atmosphere of the courtroom was very gloomy. The crowd (❷) Shylock, but nobody wanted him to be killed. When the Duke walked in, everyone(❷) very quiet.

❶ next morning: xt 發音是 /kst/，三個吐氣音相連，讀起來非常無力，因此在連接下一個字時，字尾 t 必須退讓，故而兩個字連續時，讀音非常近似 /ks/，甚至三個字母只聽得出頓音。又如：last day，其中 last 的 t 也退讓，由字首 d 來發音。

❷ hated: 這個字發音時，因為 a 是長母音，後面接著的短母音讀音很輕，而子音也必然隨之讀音很輕，故而 ed 的讀音是含在嘴裡，聽起來只有些微停頓。此外，英文發音有一個通則，就是除了少數特例，一般從字母 e 倒數第三個字母若是母音，則該母音發原音。例如 hate, late, name, became 等。

❸ became: 這個字的重音在 ca，且 a 是長母音，而長母音前後的短母音讀音都比較輕，因此 be 的 e 讀起來是含在口中，近似不發音，如同 /bkeim/。

4 Listening Comprehension

🎧42 **A** Listen to the CD and fill in the blanks.

1. There lived a _____ named Shylock in Venice.

2. Antonio often didn't _____ his fellow merchants interest.

3. Bassanio _____ the gifts into a carriage.

4. The musician began to play _____ music.

5. Shylock had nothing but _____ in his heart for these two Christians.

🎧43 **B** True or False

T F 1 ....

T F 2 ....

T F 3 ....

🎧44 **C** Write down the questions that may give the following three choices to each question .

❶ _____?

    (a) Because Antonio was married to Shylock's daughter.

    (b) Because Shylock had no money.

    (c) Because Antonio thought that Shylock was evil.

2 _____?

    (a) It is like the gentle rain falling from heaven.

    (b) It is like a golden wedding ring.

    (c) It is like a sharp knife.

3 _____?

    (a) Because he didn't have a scale.

    (b) Because he couldn't take any of Antonio's blood.

    (c) Because he didn't have a doctor.

🎧45 **D** Listen to the CD and complete the sentences.

1. _____ on the Adriatic Sea.

2. _____, he would find the picture.

3. Antonio had yelled at Shylock _____ _____.

4. On the day of trial, _____ _____.

5. That night, _____ _____.

115

Translation

　　威廉‧莎士比亞（William Shakespeare, 1564–1616），出生於英國的中產家庭，是世界上最偉大的劇作家。莎士比亞的童年因家境富裕而安逸舒適，然而十三歲時卻家道中落而未能念大學。

　　十八歲時他與長他八歲的安‧海瑟薇（Anne Hathaway）結婚，育有三子。

　　據説莎士比亞約在 1590 年開始成為劇作家。一開始，他只複寫他人的故事，鍛鍊寫作技巧，但他日漸出名，最終以演員與劇作家的身份獲得成功，並在 1594 年成為皇家官方劇團的成員，在此持續寫作直至終老。

　　他著有 37 個劇本，作品被廣泛分為四個時期：歷史劇時期、「歡樂」（joyous）喜劇時期、悲劇時期與悲劇浪漫喜劇時期。他著名的四大悲劇為《哈姆雷特》（Hamlet）、《奧賽羅》（Othello）、《李爾王》（King Lear）與《馬克白》（Macbeth），寫於悲劇時期。莎劇中的十四行詩使他享有詩人之首的頭銜，及有史以來最偉大劇作家的名聲。

　　1616 年 4 月 23 日，莎士比亞在 52 歲生日當天於出生地史特拉福（Stratford-Upon-Avon）去世，當地居民至今仍年年為其冥誕慶祝。

　　《威尼斯商人》是 1597 年出版的喜劇，共五幕。威尼斯商人安東尼奧有個名為巴薩尼奧的摯友。某一天，巴薩尼奧問安東尼奧借錢，因為他極度需要錢好向住在貝爾蒙特的波蒂亞求愛。安東尼奧雖然答應，卻無法自己借出款項，只好向放貸者夏洛克以極高的利率借款。如果無法如時還錢，夏洛克甚至可以要得安東尼奧一磅的肉。

　　為了求娶波蒂亞，巴薩尼奧首先得從三個由金、銀、鉛製成的不同箱子中，選出其中裝有波蒂亞畫像的那個。他通過測試而得到迎娶她的機會。

　　這時，安東尼奧的船隻全數沉沒，還不出錢給夏洛克。機智的波蒂亞聽聞此事便喬裝成男人，成為安東尼奧的律師，最終以智慧拯救了他。

　　她提醒夏洛克，由於合約上沒有允許見血，除非能滴血不流，否則不得割走安東尼奧一磅的肉。

　　《威尼斯商人》是莎士比亞的浪漫喜劇之一，也是所有喜劇中最受歡迎、最成功的作品。

夏洛克

我是做放貸的，住在義大利的威尼斯。我把錢貸給別人，收取高利，從中大賺了不少錢。威尼斯的人民仇視我，因為我是一位貪婪的猶太人。但我無所謂，況且我也討厭他們，尤其最討厭安東尼奧。

安東尼奧

我跟夏洛克一樣，也是在做放貸的，不過我們很不一樣。我樂於幫助有難的人，我借錢給別人，往往不收取絲毫利息。夏洛克因此對我大為不滿，而我也很不喜歡他，因為他為人冷酷又貪心。

巴薩尼奧

我是安東尼奧最好的朋友。只要我缺錢，他就會幫我。最近，我和一位窈窕淑女波蒂亞相戀，所以需要錢買些禮物來向她求婚。一如往常，我會去求助於安東尼奧。

波蒂亞

我的父親最近剛過世，因此繼承了大筆遺產。他在臨終前，對想娶我的追求者開了一些條件，求婚者必須通過一項試驗。

葛提諾和娜麗莎

我們是巴薩尼奧和波蒂亞的僕人。雖然我們出身低微，但他們待我們如家人，我們會永遠對他們忠心耿耿。

[第一章] 放貸的人

p. 14–15 我要說一個故事,這是個愛與恨的故事,一個施與受的故事,一個笑與淚的故事。這個故事在許久以前就有人講述了,但是時至今日一樣意味深長。故事發生在義大利一個叫作威尼斯的城市,這個美麗的城市,宛如一顆皇冠上的珠寶,鑲嵌在亞得里亞海上。

威尼斯城裡住著一個名叫夏洛克的放貸者,他靠著借錢給商人而賺了很多錢。許多人憎恨夏洛克。有些人憎恨他,是因為他迫使商人用很悽慘的方式償還借款;其他人憎恨他,只因為他是猶太人。

p. 16–17 在所有住在威尼斯的商人當中,有一個人最憎恨夏洛克,他的名字叫安東尼奧。

夏洛克也憎恨安東尼奧,這是因為安東尼奧是個非常慷慨的放貸者。他借錢給有困難的人,而且經常不收利息。因為安東尼奧的寬宏大量,夏洛克失去了許多生意。

更重要的是,夏洛克憎恨安東尼奧是因為他是基督徒;而安東尼奧憎恨夏洛克,則是因為他是猶太人。在那個年頭,猶太人和基督徒彼此老看不對眼,他們凡事都無法取得共識,也難以理解對方的宗教或文化。

安東尼奧和夏洛克常常在里艾爾托巧遇。里艾爾托是威尼斯的商業中心,這兩個人一見面就會起爭執。安東尼奧經常對夏洛克大聲吼叫,指責他做生意的方式冷酷無情。夏洛克則常常思索報復安東尼奧的法子。

p. 18-19 在威尼斯，幾乎人人由衷喜歡安東尼奧。他們覺得他寬厚又誠實。商人尤其讚佩他。他們知道，當他們生意困難時，他會幫助他們。

安東尼奧最要好的朋友，是一個名叫巴薩尼奧的年輕人。巴薩尼奧的家族非常富有，他的父母曾給他錢，但是巴薩尼奧全把它花個精光，把錢都揮霍在美酒和佳餚上了。他出外旅行，玩得很開心。而當然，到末了他一文不名。這在當時是年輕男子非常普遍的現象。

過去，安東尼奧曾在許多方面幫助過他。事實上，他已經欠了安東尼奧很多錢。

安東尼奧對巴薩尼奧從不說「不」字。看起來，安東尼奧似乎樂於跟朋友們分享錢財。

p. 20-21 一天，巴薩尼奧又來找安東尼奧借錢。

「安東尼奧！我有個大好消息！我愛上了一個人！她名叫波蒂亞。她是世上最美麗的女人！不僅如此，她還很有錢。她父親不久前去世了，她將繼承一大筆財富！」

「這真是好消息，巴薩尼奧。」安東尼奧說：「聽起來，她是個很棒的女子，但是，她一如你愛她一樣地愛你嗎？」

「當然囉。當她看著我時，眼神充滿了愛和尊敬。聽我說啊，我想買一些禮物送給她。唯一的問題是，我現在身無分文。我知道我欠你很多錢，但是我可不可以再借一些？我保證會還你。」

p. 22-23 「巴薩尼奧！你知道的，我的錢就是你的錢。任何時候我都會欣然借錢給你。唯一的問題是我現在也沒有錢。我把錢都拿去買貨了，幫不了你，對不起。」

「我該怎麼辦？」巴薩尼奧問道：「要是我不給送她一

些禮物，她決不會嫁給我的。」

「別擔心，」安東尼奧說：「我知道你可以怎麼做。你可以向一個名叫夏洛克的放貸者借錢，他手頭上都有錢。如果我簽下一紙借據的話，他一定會借錢給你。而且商船現在隨時會進港，等貨運到了，我就會大賺一筆，到時就有錢還給他了。」

「謝了，安東尼奧。你真是個夠意思的朋友！」

p. 24-25 就在巴薩尼奧和安東尼奧出去找夏洛克之際，波蒂亞正面臨她自己的難題。波蒂亞的父親在臨終前，已安排好了她結婚的條件。

他不信任波蒂亞的判斷力，他覺得她會選擇一個不適合的對象結婚。所以，他在臨終前放了三口箱子在一個房間裡。一口箱子是金子做的，一口是銀子做的，還有一口是鉛做的。其中一口箱子裡有一幅波蒂亞的小畫像。

求婚者若選對了箱子就會找到畫像，表示他可以向波蒂亞求婚。波蒂亞的父親相信，最佳的丈夫會知道要選哪一口箱子。

而如果他找錯了箱子，他就必須立刻離開大宅，不可以娶波蒂亞，而且餘生都不能夠娶任何人或交女朋友。每一位求婚者都必須簽下一紙契約，同意這些條件。這對他們而言，是很大的風險。但是波蒂亞的父親覺得，他的女兒值得這項風險。

p. 26-27 波蒂亞住在一個叫作貝爾蒙特的小鎮上，她讓許多男士前來造訪她的宅邸。他們都想要娶她，因為她既富有又美麗。她厭煩了讓這些陌生男子來她家，也很難過，因為她的父親不信任她的判斷力。波蒂亞常常跟僕人娜麗莎談到她的煩惱。娜麗莎比較像是朋友，不像個僕人。

「我父親為什麼不能就信任我？」
有一天她問娜麗莎。

　　「妳父親是對的，」娜麗莎說：「外
面有太多壞男人，他們只是為了妳的錢，
才想要娶妳。」

　　「可是來這裡的男人都好無趣。他們沒禮貌，而且又虛
榮。有的喝酒過量，有的還抽菸！啊！我真是厭惡這些傢伙！」

p. 28–29 波蒂亞是個非常獨立的人，她有能力自己作決定，也
認為自己的頭腦比大多數男人都好。波蒂亞感到悲歎，她覺
得她會被迫嫁給一個乏味、愚蠢又有惡習的男人。

　　「這些傢伙沒一個是正派的，我該怎麼辦？」

　　「妳還記得那個來自威尼斯的男人嗎？」娜麗莎問道。

　　波蒂亞眼眸閃爍著光輝。「是啊，我記得他。巴薩尼奧，
我怎麼可能忘記？他比其他所有來這兒的男人都強多了，既
英俊又溫文；他迷人、和善又聰穎。但那是無望的！他決不
會簽下我父親的契約。我是個連選擇自己丈夫都辦不到的女
人。我實在太不幸了！」

　　這時另一名僕人進入房間。

　　「小姐，摩洛哥王子捎來了信息，他明天會抵達。」

　　「好極了！又是一個不適合的追求者！不知這個會有什
麼毛病。」

了解故事背景：威尼斯

p. 32–33 威尼斯城的建立始於西元 452 年。當時異族入侵義
大利北部，居住在該區各城市的羅馬人，於是撤遷至位於亞
得里亞海岸外不遠處的數百座小島上。

他們用所謂「椿」的木樑，來搭築住屋和其他建築物。為了連接各個小島，建造了數百座橋。這些橋多數建成拱形，好讓船隻可從橋下通過，因而威尼斯的許多「街道」其實是水道。

西元 697 年，這些倖存的羅馬人成立了一個共和國。政府鼓勵商業，於是很快地，威尼斯便發展成一個重要的商業中樞。

今日，拜那些形成其諸多街道的運河之賜，威尼斯已是個舉世聞名的觀光勝地。一條條稱作「貢多拉」的平底遊覽船，載著人們從城內的一區到另一區。威尼斯的商業精神，如今猶活在繁忙的里艾爾托市場內，在那兒，觀光客可找到各式各樣的廉價商品。

[第二章] 借貸

p. 34-35 這時，在威尼斯，安東尼奧和巴薩尼奧找到了夏洛克。一如往常，他在里艾爾托。

「夏洛克，我要拜託你一件事。」安東尼奧說：「我想要你借三千達卡幣給我的摯友巴薩尼奧。我會在借契上簽字，數日之內，我就會欣然償還你。等我的船隻抵達，我就會有一大筆錢了。」

「我有個主意。」巴薩尼奧說：「我們何不出去吃個晚餐？我們可以詳談這筆貸款的細節。」

「我從不跟基督徒共餐，」夏洛克語帶不滿地說：「我也許會借錢給他們，或是跟他們做生意，但是我不跟他們一起吃飯。決不！」

「好吧，」巴薩尼奧說：「那麼，你要不就乾脆把錢借給我？你知道的，安東尼奧會償還你的。」

p. 36-37 夏洛克聽著安東尼奧和巴薩尼奧說的話，心裡越來越憤怒。這兩個男人是多麼愚蠢哪！他們明知道他憎恨他們，卻還開口向他借錢！他決心要讓安東尼奧付出昂貴的代價。

「夏洛克！」安東尼奧吼道：「你到底借不借我們錢？回答我！」

　　夏洛克慢吞吞地回答：「你還記得有好多次你用大家都聽得到的嗓門侮辱我吧？有一次你吐我口水，還罵我是一條狗，而現在你卻要向我這條狗，借錢！」

　　「聽著！我不是要請你幫忙。你想要跟我收多少利息都行，我不介意。我的船現在隨時都會抵達。」

　　「好，安東尼奧，我願意把錢借給你，甚至不會跟你要一分利息，只要你準時把借款還給我。」

p. 38–39 安東尼奧無法相信他的耳朵。「你說什麼？」

　　「我說你不了解我，你老是罵我是個吝嗇鬼，但我不是。我會幫你的忙，甚至不會向你索取一文達卡。不過，萬一你不還我錢呢？」

　　「別擔心，夏洛克，我會還你的。」

　　「這個嘛，我需要某種保證，是吧？三千達卡幣，可是一筆大數目啊。要是你不準時還給我，我就要一磅肉，我要從你身上隨便哪個部位取下一磅肉。」

　　安東尼奧不喜歡夏洛克提出的條件。「不行。要是我還款遲了，我寧願付一些利息。」

　　「恐怕不行。」夏洛克笑著說道：「你以為，我會向一個放貸的同業拿利息錢嗎？再說，這份契約只是個玩笑！你以為有哪個律師或法官會相信我？他們真的會相信我要你身上的一磅肉嗎？這只是我的表達方式，意思是，我們之間以往的恩怨一筆勾銷了。」

p. 40–41 安東尼奧把巴薩尼奧拉到一旁，私下跟他說話。

　　「我不想跟這個人做生意了，他很壞。而且我知道，要是他辦得到，他會從我身上取下一磅肉。我們看看有沒有別人肯借我們這筆錢吧。」

但是巴薩尼奧另有看法。「在威尼斯，還有誰有能力借我這麼多錢？何況，這個人瘋了。別擔心這項保證，沒有人會讓你付出一磅肉的！人人都會認為他是個瘋子！」

於是，安東尼奧同意了貸款的條件，三人去找了一名律師簽下契約。

夏洛克的臉上泛過一抹奇異的微笑。其實，夏洛克想要安東尼奧身上的一磅肉，長久以來他就憎恨安東尼奧，就因為這個寬大慷慨的放貸者，害他損失了好多錢。

p. 42–43 巴薩尼奧拿了安東尼奧在對借款契約有不祥預感下所借來的錢。

他買了許多要向波蒂亞求婚所需的禮物和衣裳，然後把禮物裝到四輪馬車上。他和僕人葛提諾駕著馬車，去到波蒂亞的住家。

巴薩尼奧抵達時，波蒂亞好開心。她曾希望他會回來找她，她愛上他了。

「波蒂亞，我好高興又見到妳了，」巴薩尼奧說道：「可是，我有一件很不好的事情要告訴妳。我破產了，一文不名了。」

「巴薩尼奧！別擔心那個！我們需要多少錢我都有，對我而言金錢毫不重要。你唯一要擔心的事是要選對箱子，然後我們就可以從此過著幸福快樂的日子了。」

波蒂亞把父親規定的契約，告訴巴薩尼奧。

p. 44–45 「好，我現在就去選箱子。」

波蒂亞開始擔憂了，萬一他選錯了箱子怎麼辦？

「不要在今天選吧，我有不祥的預感，我要你再等等。」

「等！可是我越早選就能越早娶妳啊，我再也等不了了。」

「那麼我來僱一位樂師來，説不定音樂會幫助你思考更清楚一些。」

　　不一會兒，樂師來了。他開始演奏舒緩的音樂，巴薩尼奧慢慢走到金箱子那兒，仔細地瞧它。

　　「不可能是這個。」他自語著：「這個選擇太明顯了，人人都會先選金箱子。我想，波蒂亞的父親，是想要區分有智慧的男人和愚蠢的男人。」

　　接著，他走到銀箱子那兒。「一般男人如果沒有選擇金箱子，那麼就會選擇這一個，這個選擇也是太明顯了。」

　　`p. 46–47` 巴薩尼奧的目光停在鉛箱子上。

　　「這是最不明顯的選擇了，我不認為還有誰會選擇這個。」

　　他打開箱子，倒抽了一口氣。他無法相信自己的眼睛！箱內有一幅波蒂亞的小畫像，巴薩尼奧現在可以娶她了！他樂得説不出話來。

　　波蒂亞伸臂擁抱他，説道：「喔，巴薩尼奧！我是世上最幸運的女人了。昨天，我還只是個擁有萬貫家財的女孩。今天，我就要成為人妻了。請收下這枚戒指，向我表示你願意接受我的求婚。戴上它，跟我承諾，你永遠不會取下它。」

　　「我也很幸運！」巴薩尼奧説：「昨天，我又窮又孤單；今天，卻即將與世上最美麗的女子結婚。我承諾，我永遠不會取下這枚戒指，除非我死了，我發誓！」

　　`p. 48–49` 那是個無比快樂的時刻。葛提諾覺得，這正是向巴薩尼奧提出一個要求的好時機。

　　「既然你就要結婚了，我也想要結婚。」

　　「喔，那太好了，」巴薩尼奧説：「可是你要娶誰啊？」

　　「我想娶娜麗莎。」

巴薩尼奧和波蒂亞感到非常驚喜。

「我都不知道妳想要結婚呢，娜麗莎，」
波蒂亞嚷道：「今天真是個大好日子！」

那天傍晚，兩對佳偶結成連理。巴薩尼奧
和葛提諾，戴著他們承諾永不取下的金戒指。
他們是世界上最快樂的男人了。

[第三章] 債

p. 52-53 數日後，一名信差抵達波蒂亞和巴薩尼奧的住家。巴薩尼奧收下信，打開它，信上寫道：

親愛的巴薩尼奧，

　　我的船隻全數沉沒了。我身陷大麻煩，夏洛克要取我身上的一磅肉。所有人都勸過他打消此舉，連威尼斯公爵都試過了，但是沒有人收到絲毫成效。

　　我就要死了，請來我的審判和行刑場吧。我想再見你一面，快來，我沒有多少時間了。

你的朋友，
安東尼奧

巴薩尼奧讀著短信，他面色轉白。他得坐下，雙手顫抖著。

p. 54-55 波蒂亞奔向他。「怎麼了？出了什麼事？拜託！回答我！」

「噢！我可憐的朋友安東尼奧！他要死了！波蒂亞，仔細聽我說，我不僅是個窮光蛋，還是個債務人。」

巴薩尼奧把借錢和一磅肉的事，一五一十都告訴了波蒂亞。

一股寒意竄過波蒂亞全身。她無法相信，一個人竟然想要割下別人身上的肉。

「巴薩尼奧，立刻去看你的朋友，」她說：「你現在是我的丈夫了，我的錢就是你的錢，你一定要償還安東尼奧的債。我會給你原本借款的兩倍金額。快去，不然安東尼奧就要被殺了。」

　　巴薩尼奧將一大筆錢，放進一個袋子裡，便動身前往威尼斯。他在監牢裡找到了安東尼奧。一看見朋友，安東尼奧奔過去擁抱他。安東尼奧看起來瘦小又虛弱。

　　「我親愛的朋友，」巴薩尼奧說道：「我今天就去找夏洛克，把錢償還他。我想他一定會把錢收下，然後你就可以自由了。畢竟，他那麼貪婪，是不會跟錢說不的。」

p.56-57 「親愛的巴薩尼奧，」安東尼奧說：「你太好心了，可是我想事情已經太遲了。夏洛克要我身上的一磅肉，依照借款契約，那正是我欠他的東西，你無法勸服他打消此意的。」

　　「他以前從來沒有拒絕過錢啊。」

　　「這次情況不同。他憎恨死我了，所以想要殺死我。而且，事情更糟的是，潔西卡離家出走了。」

　　「潔西卡？你是指夏洛克的女兒嗎？」

　　「沒錯。她嫁給了那個住在你父母家的年輕人，那個基督徒青年。她打算放棄她的宗教信仰成為基督徒，而且她逃家時，還偷走了夏洛克一顆寶石。」

　　「噢，那太糟糕了。」巴薩尼奧說。

　　「他八成認為是我讓她嫁給那個基督徒，可是我跟那件事毫無關係，我發誓！他真的瘋了！他把潔西卡從遺囑中除名了，而且過去這幾天夏洛克老在談論我，他逢人就說要殺了我。」

p. 58-59 「別擔心那個。」巴薩尼奧說:「我會跟夏洛克談,我會讓他改變心意。只要是必須做的,無論什麼我都會去做。」

巴薩尼奧離開了監牢,找到夏洛克。

「拜託,我求你,請饒了安東尼奧的命吧。拜託,請將他從監牢釋放了吧。這裡有六千達卡幣,這是我們當初向你借的金額的兩倍。」巴薩尼奧跪地懇求。

「不行,我要一磅肉,那是他欠我的。」

「我願意給你九千達卡幣。只求你放他活命!」

「不行。」

「你開價吧,任何數目我都願意付給你。」

「我要一磅肉。」

巴薩尼奧明白夏洛克不會改變心意了,他能做的只有一件事,他必須上法院。

p. 60-61 當時,全威尼斯的人都在談論這個麻煩問題。人人都為安東尼奧感到難過,他只是想要幫助朋友啊。而且人人憎惡夏洛克,他這個人真邪惡。然而,他的憤怒更甚於邪惡。

夏洛克對安東尼奧十分憤怒。安東尼奧在里艾爾托跟他說話時,總是粗暴無禮。他曾因為夏洛克是猶太人而詛咒他;他曾大聲叫罵夏洛克是個吝嗇貪婪的生意人。

夏洛克對他女兒的事也非常生氣,他的整個世界是一片黑暗不潔的可憎之地,因而心中對安東尼奧和巴薩尼奧這兩個基督徒只有憎恨。

開庭審判的日期決定了。這是一場非常重要的審判,連威尼斯公爵都涉入其中了,他將擔任主審法官。

p. 62-63 此時,在貝爾蒙特的波蒂亞聽說了審判之事。她思考後決定要幫助可憐的安東尼奧,她不能倚靠命運來決定事件的發展。

波蒂亞寫了一封信給表哥貝拉里奧，他是一位非常知名的律師。她徵詢他對安東尼奧這件案子的意見，還請他把他在法庭上穿的衣服借給她。

　　數日後，一封信和一口箱子寄達貝爾蒙特。信上寫著替安東尼奧作辯護的重點指示。箱子裡是兩套貝拉里奧在法庭上穿的衣服。

　　波蒂亞穿上其中一套，並讓娜麗莎穿上另一套，便動身前往威尼斯。

　　波蒂亞和娜麗莎去到威尼斯大法院，在那兒等待開庭。審判當天，似乎所有威尼斯人都到了法院。人人都想要知道，安東尼奧會遭遇什麼下場。

了解故事背景：夏洛克——他真的是那麼壞的人嗎？

`p. 66–67` 有些人曾批評《威尼斯商人》把猶太人寫得很壞。然而，也有人反駁說，莎士比亞只是用歷史事實，來創造他的戲劇角色。

　　在他寫這齣戲劇的年代，威尼斯是個商業化的基督教城市。像安東尼奧和巴薩尼奧這樣的年輕基督徒，可以藉由投資船業，載運珍貴貨物往返地中海來致富。

　　不過，要賺錢，首先你得有錢。基督徒認為，借錢給別人索取利息是「惡」的，因而基督徒沒有財務理由去借錢給別人。

　　然而，猶太教並沒有任何教規禁止索取利息。而且有時放貸還是猶太人在基督教的商業世界中，養活自己和家人的唯一方法。因此許多猶太人，就像夏洛克，以放貸索利為業。這正是許多基督徒認為猶太人貪婪的原因。

　　夏洛克被視為貪婪的人。不幸的是，這一點反映出對中古時期和現代猶太人的一種常見的刻版印象。所以，他真的是那麼壞的人嗎？你認為呢？

[第四章] 審判

p. 68–69 審判剛開始，波蒂亞就呈交一封信給威尼斯公爵。信是貝拉里奧寫的，信上說，他因病而無法擔任安東尼奧的律師。

貝拉里奧寫道，包特哈薩將替代他擔任安東尼奧的律師。包特哈薩其實是波蒂亞喬裝的，公爵並不在意他將代表安東尼奧作辯護。不過，他真懷疑包特哈薩的經驗是否夠老道。「他」看起來非常年輕。

波蒂亞環視偌大的法庭。夏洛克似乎正享受著他的出庭日，安東尼奧用哀懇的目光看著她。波蒂亞接著望向她的丈夫，巴薩里奧也沒有發覺，包特哈薩其實就是他的妻子。

p. 70–71 開庭了，法庭內安靜了下來。波蒂亞首先對夏洛克說話。

「先生，依照借貸契約，您可以從安東尼奧身上取下一磅肉，這一點毫無疑問，但是我想要提醒您還有另一個選擇，一個更高尚的選擇。

您可以選擇慈悲。您或許會問：『何謂慈悲？』這個嘛，我來告訴您。慈悲就像溫柔的細雨，從天而降，賜福眾生。它賜福施予慈悲的人，也賜福受到慈悲的人。慈悲，使您感覺自己像是個國王，擁有世界上一切的權力。您擁有給予安東尼奧性命的權力，而唯有經由慈悲，您才能做到這一點。」

法庭內所有市民一致同意波蒂亞的話。每一個人，只除了夏洛克。

「我不在乎慈悲！我只要司法正義！」他吼道。

p. 72–73 「唔，那您何不就讓安東尼奧，把借款償還給您呢？」

「現在償還已經太遲了，我不要錢，我要我的一磅肉。讀讀借契，上面言明，我可以取這一磅肉。契約上還說了，我可以從最靠近他心臟的部位取下這一磅肉。」

「那麼，安東尼奧，您必須準備受死了。」波蒂亞說。
眾人個個倒抽一口氣，他們無法相信自己聽到的話。

「夏洛克，」波蒂亞用懇求的聲音說道：「請求您，收
下還款，讓我撕掉借契吧。」

夏洛克說：「我絕不會改變心意，什麼理由都沒用。」

他開始磨利他的長刀，等不及要將長刀插入安東尼奧的
身體。

p. 74–75 波蒂亞轉向安東尼奧。「您有什麼遺言嗎？」

「沒有，」安東尼奧說道：「我已準備好受死了。」

然後他轉向巴薩尼奧。「別了，我的朋友，不要為我的
死而自責。」

巴薩尼奧哭了。「噢，安東尼奧，我願意
做任何事來挽救你的生命，可是我毫無辦法，
我好對不起。你是世界上最好的朋友。」

「說夠了，」夏洛克吼道：「咱們繼續吧，
我要我的一磅肉。」

波蒂亞詢問公爵：「磅秤準備好了嗎？」公爵頷首，
「醫生到場了嗎？」

「什麼醫生？」夏洛克問道。

「庭內應該有一位醫生，安東尼奧不應流血至死。」

但是，當然，夏洛克想要他流血至死。

「契約上隻字未提要有一位醫生在場啊。」

「可是無疑地，我們需要有一位醫生在場，唯有這樣做
才正當！」

p. 76–77 「契約上隻字未提要有一位醫生在場啊。」夏洛克再
說一遍。

　　「好吧，」波蒂亞説：「一磅肉是您的了，這是法律允許的，法庭裁定的。」

　　夏洛克非常高興，因為終於可以殺死仇敵了。他十分滿意這位年輕的律師。

　　「你真是一位出色的律師，」他説：「你懂得正義。」

　　夏洛克拿起他的利刃，長刀閃閃發亮，這放貸者的眼睛中有種邪惡的神色。

　　「過來，」他對安東尼奧説。

　　「且慢，」波蒂亞説道：「還有一件事情我必須告訴您，這份契約並未言明您可以得到任何一滴血。假使安東尼奧損失了一滴血，您就觸法了。威尼斯市政府將沒收您的所有錢財和土地。您明白嗎？」

p. 78–79 夏洛克不知要説什麼才好，情勢完全改觀了。現在不可能報復得逞了，他氣得臉面漲紅。

　　法庭內人人佩服這位年輕律師，「包特哈薩」運用契約條款解救了安東尼奧。契約並未提到血，夏洛克不能取走一滴血，故而他也無法取下任何一塊肉。

　　法庭內眾人鼓起掌來。「包特哈薩萬歲！」

　　夏洛克用拳頭猛捶一下桌子。

　　「哼，那我的錢呢？要是不能拿到我的一磅肉，那我就要我的錢。」

　　「拿去吧。」巴薩尼奧欣然將一個裝著三千達卡幣的袋子扔給他。夏洛克起步欲離去。

p. 80–81 「別走得那麼快，」波蒂亞説：「你意圖謀害別人，依法，你必須把你所有的錢財交給威尼斯市。你也可以被處死，你得聽憑威尼斯公爵的處置，跪地向他求饒吧。」

「不，」公爵說道：「我認為人不該向別人求饒，這是不對的。我得作出一項重要的決定，我要仔細思考一番。我裁定今晚把夏洛克扔進監牢，明天我會告訴你們要如何懲罰他。」

那天下午大家都離開了法院，他們穿過街道時還聊著審判，沒人想得起還有哪天比這天更不尋常的了。

[第五章] 判決

p. 84–85 次日早晨，天色陰沉，還下著雨。夏洛克覺得，那是他生命的最後一日了。法庭裡氣氛鬱悶消沉。眾人憎惡夏洛克，但是沒人想要他被處死。

當公爵步入法庭，人群頓時鴉雀無聲。

「大多數人都懂得慈悲，」公爵開口說話：「而你，夏洛克，似乎並不懂得慈悲。我是一個凡人，我懂得慈悲，也懂得人命的價值。秉諸慈悲的精神，我寬恕你。我要饒了你的命，不過，我必須懲罰你。如果我不這麼做，許多人會有樣學樣。你必須將你一半的錢財給安東尼奧，另一半給威尼斯市。」

p. 86–87 安東尼奧素來是個慷慨寬大之人，即使發生了這一切依舊如此。他知道夏洛克的女兒潔西卡很窮。

「對於這筆錢，我有一個請求，」安東尼奧說。

「你有什麼請求？」公爵問道。

法庭內再度鴉雀無聲，眾人傾身向前聆聽。

「我想要把夏洛克的錢送給他的女兒，而且我要他把潔西卡重新寫入他的遺囑內。」

「我認為這是一個公道的請求。夏洛克，我命令你，把你的錢財半數給潔西卡，還有你一定要把她重新寫入你的遺囑內。如果你不這樣做，我就把你扔進監牢，讓你在牢中度過餘生。」

夏洛克心生惱怒，他未能報復安東尼奧，又失去了錢財。他憎恨每個人。

「行，我會照您的意思做，只要立刻放了我。我身體有點不舒服。」

夏洛克獲得釋放，穿過街頭還還扯著頭髮，他無法相信自己的運氣！

p. 88–89 「先生，」公爵對波蒂亞說：「我這輩子從未見過如此聰明的律師。我要承認起初我還很擔心，因為你看起來實在太年輕了。如果你不太忙的話，今晚請與我共餐，我很想跟你談談法律。」

波蒂亞想要趕在丈夫之前先到家。「我很樂意，可是我還有另一件案子要花工夫研究，抱歉啊，我實在太忙，今晚無法與您共餐。」

「噢，是這樣啊，那就改天吧。」

公爵轉向安東尼奧：「你該好好地酬謝他，你欠他太多啦。」

「請你，」巴薩尼奧對波蒂亞說：「收下這三千達卡吧，這是我們當初向夏洛克借貸的數額。」

「我不要這筆錢。」

「那麼，我再多給你三千。」

「我一毛錢也不要，」波蒂亞說。「我比較想要你的婚戒。」

p. 90–91 「我的婚戒？對不起。這是世界上我唯一不能給你的東西。我向內人承諾永遠不會取下它。我願意找全威尼斯最昂貴的戒指，立刻買下來送給你，就是不能給你這枚戒指，絕對不行。」

「我要你的婚戒，可是我不打算求你。我看你是太吝嗇，所以不肯把它給我。」

波蒂亞離開了法庭，她狀似生氣，其實很高興。

「拜託，巴薩尼奧，把戒指給他吧。」安東尼奧説。

「我知道你的妻子會生氣，可是想想這位律師今天為我們做的事，我欠他這條命啊，難道你不認為這一點值得你的婚戒嗎？」

巴薩尼奧感到羞慚，安東尼奧説得對。他取下婚戒，交給葛提諾。

「去，找到包特哈薩，把這枚戒指給他。」

葛提諾找到了波蒂亞，把戒指給她。跟她在一起的娜麗莎説道：「你！葛提諾！你也把你的戒指給我。」

葛提諾知道自己不能説不字，也把戒指給了她。

p. 92–93 待波蒂亞和娜麗莎獨處時，她倆大笑一場，她們決定要捉弄她們的丈夫。

這天傍晚，巴薩尼奧和葛提諾返回貝爾蒙特。他們看到妻子正等著他們，兩人親吻了妻子。一時之間，大家都因再度重聚而幸福洋溢。

不久，兩個女人開始對他們吼叫。

「你的婚戒到哪兒去了？」波蒂亞喊道。

「你們把我們的婚戒給了別的女人。」娜麗莎尖叫。

「請相信我們，」巴薩尼奧説：「我們把戒指給了兩位年輕的律師，那兩位律師救了我至友的性命。他們説要我們的婚戒當做律師費，就是不肯接受任何其他的酬勞。請諒解，親愛的，他們救了安東尼奧的命！」

巴薩尼奧感到難過又愧疚。

p. 94-95 「我看我們只有一個法子了。」波蒂亞説。巴薩尼奧心驚膽顫，葛提諾雙膝顫抖。

「我們只好把你們的戒指還給你們了。」

波蒂亞張開她的手心，娜麗莎也是。巴薩尼奧和葛提諾無法相信自己的眼睛！她倆手裡握著他們的婚戒！

波蒂亞和娜麗莎吃吃笑了起來，越笑越厲害。兩個男人站在那兒，滿臉困惑不解的神情。

終於，波蒂亞開始講述她們的事。巴薩尼奧驚異不已，他的妻子比他想得還要棒。她是全義大利最聰明的女人，她救了他至友的性命。他喜不自勝。

p. 96-97 彷彿這個驚喜還不夠似的，不久，一名信差又帶來了另一個驚喜。那人送來的消息説，安東尼奧的船隻並未沉沒，船已經安然抵達威尼斯，貨品隨時可以出售了。他們開心極了。

這天晚上，他們一塊在美麗的義大利月光下慶祝。想到戒指，以及波蒂亞和娜麗莎捉弄巴薩尼奧和葛提諾的把戲，他們開懷大笑。

巴薩尼奧疼愛地看著妻子。

「什麼是世界上最可怕的事？」他問她。

「欠放貸者一磅肉？」波蒂亞問道。

「絕對不是！是丟掉我妻子的婚戒。」

巴薩尼奧從此再也沒有取下他的戒指。

Answers

P. 30

A
1. arguments
2. religion
3. loan
4. merchandise
5. decisions

B
1. Antonio
2. Portia
3. Nerissa
4. Bassanio

P. 31

C
1. (c)
2. (b)

D
1. - b
2. - a
3. - c

P. 50

A
1. F
2. T
3. F
4. T
5. T

B
1. borrowed
2. hated
3. nothing
4. wrong

P. 51

C
1. (b)
2. (c)

D
1. How beautiful she is!
2. What a handsome man he is!
3. What a big house they have!
4. How tall the trees are!

P. 64

A
1. F
2. T
3. T
4. F
5. F

B
4 → 1 → 2 → 5 → 3

P. 65

C
1. (a)
2. (c)

D
1. evil
2. change
3. cursed
4. opinion
5. instructions

P. 82

A
1. - d
2. - c
3. - b
4. - a

B
1. F
2. T
3. T
4. F

P. 83　C　❶ represent　❷ blesses　❸ sharpening
　　　　　 ❹ break　❺ murder

　　　　D　❶ - ⓓ　❷ - ⓐ　❸ - ⓒ　❹ - ⓑ

P. 98　A　❷ → ❸ → ❶ → ❺ → ❹

　　　　B　❶ atmosphere　❷ value　❸ revenge
　　　　　 ❹ payment　❺ happiness

P. 99　C　❶ (c)　❷ (b)

　　　　D　❶ Shylock　❷ The Duke　❸ Antonio　❹ Nerissa

P. 114　A　❶ moneylender　❷ charge　❸ loaded
　　　　　 ❹ soothing　❺ hatred

　　　　B　❶ Portia's father had put three chests in a room before he died. (T)
　　　　　 ❷ Shylock lent six thousand ducats to Bassanio. (F)
　　　　　 ❸ Balthasar was actually Portia in disguise. (T)

　　　　C　❶ Why did Antonio not want to do business with Shylock? (c)
　　　　　 ❷ What did Balthasar say about mercy? (a)
　　　　　 ❸ How come Shylock couldn't take a pound of flesh from Antonio? (b)

P. 115　D　❶ This beautiful city rests like a crown jewel
　　　　　 ❷ If a suitor chose the right box
　　　　　 ❸ for being a mean and greedy businessman
　　　　　 ❹ it seemed like every Venetian came to the court
　　　　　 ❺ they all celebrated under the beautiful moon

Adaptor of *The Merchant of Venice*

David Desmond O'Flaherty

University of Carleton (Honors English Literature and Language)
Kwah-Chun Foreign Language High School,
English Conversation Teacher

威尼斯商人【二版】
The Merchant of Venice

作者 _ 莎士比亞（William Shakespeare）
改寫 _ David Desmond O'Flaherty
插圖 _ Gutdva Irina Mixailovna
翻譯 _ 王啥
編輯 _ 黃鈺云
作者 / 故事簡介翻譯 _ 王采翎
校對 _ 賴祖兒
封面設計 _ 林書玉
排版 _ 葳豐 / 林書玉
製程管理 _ 洪巧玲

發行人 _ 周均亮
出版者 _ 寂天文化事業股份有限公司
電話 _ +886-2-2365-9739
傳真 _ +886-2-2365-9835
網址 _ www.icosmos.com.tw
讀者服務 _ onlineservice@icosmos.com.tw
出版日期 _ 2019年11月 二版一刷（250201）
郵撥帳號 _ 1998620-0 寂天文化事業股份有限公司

國家圖書館出版品預行編目資料

威尼斯商人 / William Shakespearem 原著；David
Desmond O'Flaherty 改寫 . -- 二版 . -- [臺北市]：
寂天文化, 2019.11
    面；   公分 . -- (Grade 3 經典文學讀本)
譯自：The merchant of Venice
ISBN 978-986-318-856-8(25K 平裝附光碟片)

1. 英語 2. 讀本
805.18   108017940